PIECES LIKE POTTERY

....

STORIES OF LOSS

AND REDEMPTION

BY DAN BURI

DJB Publishing
Portland, Oregon

Book Layout ©2013 BookDesignTemplates.com
Cover Photo ©2014 David Mattox (DavidMattox.com)
Cover Design ©2015 DJB Publishing

Ordering Information:
Quantity sales. Special discounts are available on quantity purchases by corporations, associations, and others. For details, contact the "Special Sales Department" at DJB Publishing.

Pieces Like Pottery/ Dan Buri. -- 1st ed.
ISBN 978-0-692-69142-7

For Sara

Elizabeth,
Thank you for your support and readership. I am grateful.

xDan Ball

"Doubt is easy. Don't be easy. Hold on to faith and hope"

CONTENTS

It will break in pieces like pottery, shattered so mercilessly that among its pieces not a fragment will be found.

–Isaiah 30:14

THE FIFTH SORROWFUL MYSTERY:

THE GRAVESITE

The headstone glistened in the early afternoon sun. A nondescript memoriam flat against the earth marked her son's resting place. Gravestones stretched in all directions. It felt like every person in the entire state must know at least one person who was buried here. Some probably knew more than one. Seven degrees of death.

I wonder how many people are visiting their own child, she thought.

Every cliché in the book applies when a parent loses their child. Things never return to the way they were after the death of a child. A parent should never have to outlive their children, should never have to watch them lowered into the ground. Losing a child is like losing your soul; even though you continue to live on the outside, on the inside you're dying. Every one of these applied, and it didn't even begin to reveal the pain and the loss of hope she felt.

Lisa looked in agitation up the path towards the parking lot. She glanced at her watch again and sighed.

"Figures," she muttered under her breath.

"Hello, Lisa," came the unexpected reply from behind her. "Good to see you."

The man smiled at her kindly as she spun around, startled. *He must have heard me grumbling,* she thought. Lisa felt terrible for falling into old habits with him—worrying, watching, waiting, and then grumbling about it all. Some habits die hard, especially when it's someone with whom you've spent decades.

"You too," she replied sheepishly.

She couldn't formulate any words beyond that. They lodged in her chest, so she just exhaled at the ground. He stood next to her and focused on his breathing. Side-by-side they stared at the ground as he put his arm around her shoulder. Squeezing her tight, he kissed the top of her head. This gesture of love—no, care—felt nice to Lisa. She pretended to be indestructible, but had long since realized she was far from it. She'd been lost inside. Alone.

"Did you see the most recent blog post?" Mike asked.

"I haven't had a chance to look today."

"It was there when I checked this morning." Lisa knew this was the reason Mike was late. Another pang of guilt for grumbling at him a moment ago came over her. She often felt bad for their marriage, their former marriage, and what had become of it.

Mike reached into his pocket and pulled out a folded sheet of paper. Slowly he unfolded it and aimlessly looking at the words on the page, he handed it to Lisa. She took it from his hands and began to read.

"Well you build it up you wreck it down, and you burn your mansion to the ground. When there's nothing left to keep you here, when you're falling behind in this big blue world."

May 24th

As I sit here preparing for a twenty-mile trip
that'll take an hour and a half because of traffic,
I'm struck by how much the little things are
what make up a man's life. Each event, and each
reaction a man has to it, influences the course of
his life. People get so disheveled because they
are delayed ten minutes by traffic, or because
they don't like what food was prepared for them,
or they don't like the work assignment they
have been given, or countless other things that
people worry about. So many wish they were
somewhere else doing something else, but they
miss what life's really about. As the wizard of
westwood would say, "Things turn out best for
those who make the best out of the way things
turn out."

Life's circumstances always throw twists and
turns. Wishing for something more brings con-
tinual disappointment. Everyone has the ability
to control their happiness by grabbing the reins
on how they think about each day and each
event. Situations turn out sour for those who
always complain about how things turn out. We
will always be affected by our own attitudes.

Every response to every action affects our character.

It's like a rock that is constantly being dripped on. The water is not pouring out; it's a constant drip. Drip. Drip. Over time the water leaves its mark. The rock will corrode from its constant impact. Each decision we make is like that water. How we respond to life's twists and turns impacts our life as forcefully as the water impacts the rock. The decision may not be visible in a man's character in a week, a month, or even a year, but his decisions change him over time. The impact can have a corrosive effect on the man's character, like the rock under the drip, drip, drip; or it can have a smooth, even effect like a stone washed from years of salty ocean water.

As I'm stuck in traffic moving slower than I can walk, I realize that how I react to unforeseen problems, what I do each moment, and what I spend my time thinking about, all impact my character and my life's direction. Life's simple moments are not wasted and unimportant. They are the foundations that shape our lives. They are the formational moments, one added upon another. At least that's how I see things. But what do I know? One thing's for sure, I guess—it's finished. That's all I have to say. Thanks for reading.

Lisa wiped a tear from her eyes. She shook her head with amazement and disappointment. Amazed by the idealism her son has...had. Disappointed in knowing this was the end. She grabbed Mike's outstretched hand and squeezed as they gazed down on their son's gravestone at their feet.

....

Mike and Lisa had been married twenty-three years, long enough to fall in and out of love at least a dozen times. Their relationship had gone through some rocky times, but they'd always stayed together. For better and worse, right?

Three years into the marriage they hit a tumultuous time. In retrospect, it was young twenty-somethings being stubborn and small-minded, but at the time it nearly broke them entirely. They separated for awhile, but they eventually worked things out. The phrasing in this particular case—worked things out—was about as apt as could be,

Lisa thought. It took a lot of hard work from both of them.

That third year was hell. Lisa remembered how she refused to speak with Mike about anything. She wouldn't budge. It was the only time she could remember Mike's soft demeanor turning cold and angry. His usually kind and soft heart closed off. Finally they agreed, before going separate ways, to try marriage counseling. It wasn't an easy experience for either of them—each session with their "marriage therapist" seemed more painful and less productive, but something kept them coming back.

There was no breakthrough session that revived everything they'd once had. No romantic moment that reignited their passion and helped them realize they'd be together forever. This wasn't the movies. Romantic comedies are meant for Saturday nights, not Tuesday morning arguments as a marriage teeters on the brink of divorce. Mike and Lisa slowly tried to allow themselves to be vulnerable again. They opened up and shared how insecure and insignificant they felt at times. After months, the love, so to speak, seemed to return. They had worked things out, as the saying goes.

If a specific moment was needed to commemorate the renewal of their love, there had been an unexceptional Wednesday months into the process of giving their marriage one last try. Lisa always thought this was a funny way to look at things— one last try. She believed that each decision she made would build upon the other to create the fabric of what she now cared about. For her *one* try, whether it was the first or last, had never accomplished anything.

On this particular Wednesday, Lisa knew how stressed Mike had been with work, so she left the office early. It felt laborious because of all the pain she'd built up inside, but she was determined. She went to the dry cleaners to pick up the suits he needed for a business trip the next week. She planned to go to the bank to make some deposits for him and then the grocery store to pick up ingredients for a special dinner she wanted to cook. As she neared the bank, however, she noticed they had given her the wrong dry cleaning.

"You've got to be kidding me!" she said out loud in her car.

Lisa turned around to drive all the way back across town. The afternoon traffic was thickening. It seemed everyone on the road that day was in driver's education—lane changes without a signal, stopping and starting without the foggiest idea of where they wanted to go, and left turns from the right hand lane. With each passing minute the frustration built inside her. With each red light, her jaw clenched. Every minute stuck in traffic caused her to sink deeper into her seat, head hanging so low she could barely see above the steering wheel.

By the time she made it back to the dry cleaners and gave the nice woman behind the counter a piece of her mind, the afternoon was over. She once again sat in traffic, this time with the end of work rush hour. She made it to bank just before it closed, but she had no time to head to the grocery store. She drove home irritated and disappointed.

As it turned out, Mike had had a similar idea. When she walked in the door, the house smelled amazing. Maybe the smell of garlic mashed potatoes and pasta brought her back to her childhood the way only fragrances seemed capable of doing. Maybe it was the stress of the day. Maybe it was her favorite James Taylor song flowing through the speakers. Maybe it was a lifetime of being scared of who she was and what other people thought. Maybe it was the over-arching fear of being vulnerable, even with her own husband because of the danger of being hurt. Maybe all of it was weighing on her at that very moment. Whatever it was, Lisa crumbled. She immediately slumped onto the couch and began sobbing.

Mike rushed to her side and put his arm around her. They sat like that for a while, Lisa sobbing and Mike alternating between wiping Lisa's tears and brushing away his own. By the time they got off the couch, they had to reheat the dinner Mike had made, but it was one of the most amazing meals they had ever eaten. They talked late into the night about their pains and fears, hopes and dreams. It felt as if they were teenagers dating again.

If there was a moment where their love was renewed, this was it.

Life is a funny thing, though. Over the years their marriage had had good months and bad months, but they had always worked to put each other's interests before their own. They thought their relationship could withstand anything life threw at them. A marriage isn't made to withstand the death of a child, however—at least not their marriage.

N ot long after Mike and Lisa had sat on that couch crying in each other's arms, they were told they weren't able to have children. After months and months of tests, doctors diagnosed Lisa with Polycistic Ovary Syndrome (PCOS) and told her she was unable to conceive a child. This news, for Lisa, was unacceptable. For some reason, she couldn't even acknowledge the diagnosis. Stubbornness has difficulty standing on the sidelines. So she sought multiple second opinions. Mike dutifully stood by. Eventually, they found a doctor who didn't believe she had PCOS. She did have ovarian cysts, he believed, but he was convinced there was a chance she could conceive, albeit a very small chance. A year, two tries with in vitro fertilization, and thousands of dollars later, Mike and Lisa were finally expecting a little boy. Nearly five years after they both said "I do," they welcomed their only child into the world.

Chris had always been wild at heart. From what seemed like the moment he was born, Mike and Lisa had great trouble keeping Chris out of it. It was almost as if he was reacting to all the caution his parents had when he was child. In their eyes, he was such a miracle, a fragile child that should have never been born. They wouldn't dare put him in danger. From the moment of conception, Mike and Lisa cared for their son with the caution of tightrope walkers. No false steps, they would think.

Chris had other plans. He danced to the beat of his own drum and never apologized for it. By the time he was six, for every cautious decision his parents made, he made three seemingly reckless decisions. He wasn't rebellious; he was just a curious and adventurous boy. His curiosity always brought Mike and Lisa new challenges. Chris forced them to learn quickly how to let go, oftentimes when their inclination was not to. When he came to them on his eighteenth birthday and told them he wasn't going to immediately enroll in college and instead would be spending time backpacking and volunteering in India, Thailand, Malaysia (and any other number of countries thousands of miles from home), Mike and Lisa weren't surprised. This may have come as a shock to other parents, but Mike and Lisa were preparing for something like this for years.

He told them he planned to continue writing on his blog, which would allow them to track his travels and his experiences. Chris had been keeping a blog for nearly a year now. He wrote about his everyday interactions and his idealistic hopes. His last entry, the night before he flew to Bangkok, was no different.

> *"Jesus don't love me, no one ever carried my load. I'm too young to feel this old."*
May 19th

I was at the grocery store the other day in the late afternoon. The post-work rush was about to hit. I hate being at any grocery store at this time of the day. As I danced through the white-washed aisles, I tried not to become agitated by the worn-out shoppers who had just left their boring desk jobs. My goal was to make it in and out as quickly as possible, but my goal was clearly futile this late in the day. When I made my way up to check out, I felt my blood pressure rising as I watched the over-weight woman at the front of the line suck down 42 ounces of something clearly not meant to be drunk in those portions. In a moment of levity, I couldn't help but think that I was very suddenly and quite literally the person in David Foster Wallace's *This Is Water*.

As I stood in that line, I had been erroneously convinced that this trip to the grocery store was all about me, when in fact it wasn't. I had been ignoring the fact that each of these hurried individuals, the same ones I found deplorable just minutes ago, were struggling, hard-working people that wanted the same thing from life as I wanted. So I made the CHOICE, right there in the checkout aisle, to look at these people as caring individuals who just wanted to be loved, to be seen for who they were and allowed to be themselves. They didn't realize how much they were annoying me with their screaming kids, bad dietary choices, and whistling. (Why do people whistle so loudly in public?!) They knew not what they were doing. Besides, I'm sure the exposed toes resting in my flip-flops were driving some other people in the store crazy too.

So instead of becoming more annoyed by the minute, I took that moment to realize I was surrounded by water. I decided to think the best of these people around me and love them, even without them knowing I was loving them. Because this was what I would want from them.

There's no mystical power that will come along and ease their burdens. No almighty god will come down from the heavens to tell them they are loved. The only people that can do that are you and me. If we don't tell each other we're amazing individuals just the way we are, no one will.

When Lisa read Chris' last entry before she drove him to the airport, she admired his idealism, as she always did. At the same time, she couldn't help but think this exact idealism that she admired was due to the fact that he was young and naïve.

"Just wait until you get older," she told him as they drove up to the airport drop-off. "You'll realize most of those people at the grocery store are, in fact, terribly annoying people. Most of them are careless and selfish."

Chris just smiled at his mother without the slightest hint of annoyance or judgment. They hopped out of the car, and he grabbed his one bag. "I love you, Mom. Don't you dare go and lose that cynicism while I'm gone. It's my life's mission to squeeze it out you!" he said as he hugged his mother tightly.

"I love you too," Lisa doted. "Are you sure this one bag is enough?"

"Yes, Mother," he sighed in return.

He tried to avoid the eye roll, but it seemed to come reflexively. This was at least the fifth time she had commented on how few things he was bringing for a trip across the world. He had clearly grown tired of the constant focus on his backpack.

"Sorry," his mother smiled sheepishly. "You know I worry about you."

Lisa paused to kiss his forehead. Then, pulling him closely for another hug, she told him again that she loved him.

"Another post should be up while I'm en route. Short and sweet," he winked at her.

Her son kissed her goodbye and then disappeared through the automatic airport doors. Like jaws opening and closing again, the doors swallowed him up. Lord knows how many times she cursed that moment. Why didn't she hug him one last time? Why did she tell him he was naïve? She loved his writing. Why couldn't she have just told him that?

....

L isa was more than just a proud mom when it came to Chris' writing. She found his words inspirational. They made her reflect on her own disposition in life. She often sat and wondered about the meaning of each blog post, marveling at the innocent wisdom of her own son. She could have done without the quotes that opened each blog entry, but it was his artistic choice, she figured.

"Why don't you credit where you're taking the quote from?" she asked him once.

"The beauty's in the words, Mom, and in the search," she remembered him saying. Then, as if pausing with levity, he continued, "Besides, you can just look it up on the google machine anyway."

She laughed at him calling the internet "the google machine." It seemed funny to her that if someone of her generation had called it the google machine, the term would have been viewed as ridiculous. She would have been laughed at for being too old and unhip, and she would have been told that she just didn't get technology. Since it was spouted by youth, however, it was somehow acceptable and adopted. This affectation amused her at the time.

Despite not appreciating the quotes that began his blog posts, Lisa always searched. His last reference on May 19th, she learned, was from someone named Caleb Fallowill. She had never heard of him and didn't particularly like the despair in the quote. She sometimes failed to grasp why Chris provided the quotes he did. They oftentimes didn't seem relevant. On the other hand, she loved the many references Chris always had throughout his writing. He was so smart and well-read that she always loved finding out what the references meant. The reference to *This Is Water* was one of those she found fascinating after she researched it more.

Why couldn't she have said this when they drove to the airport? Why couldn't she have told him one last time how wonderful of a son he was?

The night after dropping Chris at the airport, she was not yet concerned with these thoughts. She went about her night like a parent always does, trying to ignore irrational fears that continually arise and hoping her son is happy. She also eagerly awaited Chris' next post.

The following morning she checked his site over her morning cup of coffee. A new entry was there. She smiled and sipped her warm drink.

"Unspoken rules of solitude wound without a trace. A lifetime of dreams roll down your face. All that we can't say is all we need to hear. When you close your eyes does the world disappear? There's something in everyone only they know."

May 20th

We never lose the biases that are intertwined in our lives. How we think and who we become are tightly wound up within our experiences and origins. As Michael Sandel argues, it is impossible to efface past experiences or family of origin from our thought processes. The moments that they have pierced me in the past, color my thinking in the present. I became a product of my mother the moment I was first placed into her arms. I am my father's son. We must first understand that these experiences, these biases, exist, before we can truly understand what is right.

Lisa scratched her head and stared at the screen. Sometimes she was unsure if her son was a lot smarter than her, and spoke far above her ability to comprehend him, or if he was merely spouting gibberish to be combative. She enjoyed it nonetheless. She envisioned his plane landing thousands of miles away as she sipped her coffee.

....

Mike reached out for Lisa's hand. She reciprocated, and they squeezed each other tightly. As they stood staring at the gravestone, Lisa could sense how alone Mike felt. The sun was shining brightly, but it felt like it only poured a cold heat about them. Lisa's eyes welled up again. Her tears never seemed to fade in the last year. There was a permanent quality to her sorrow that failed to grow weary.

The tears filled up to the point where Lisa's eyes could no longer contain them anymore, and began to run down her cheek one by one.

"He was such a good boy," Mike sighed.

"Such a good man," Lisa corrected through wet eyes.

Her little Chris had ventured out into the world on his own. He had wanted to see the world and save everyone in it. Such a silly idea from a young boy, but as she looked at his grave, Lisa couldn't help but think that he was more a man than she ever had given him credit for. She didn't know if she now viewed his idealism as a profound truth that she should be trying to practice in her own life, or if she just wanted it to be so because he was no longer by her side.

"Such a good *man*," Mike mirrored with an air of satisfaction.

A week after Chris took that flight to Thailand, he called his parents at home. He raved about the first week of the trip. He had already met so many interesting people. As his mother worried about him being all alone, Chris couldn't stop expressing how excited he was to be out on his own. Things felt right. His father told him he was proud of his son, such independence and adventure in his heart. Then Chris cut the call short to head out with an acquaintance he'd just met for a hike into the jungle to see a waterfall. He was in Ko Pha Ngan. That was the last time they spoke to their son.

Authorities were unable to find his body. They said he must have slipped off a cliff ledge and fell into the river below. They suspected he'd died before he'd hit the water, bouncing off the jagged cliff walls that jutted out awkwardly. He was with another American boy who was on a post-high school tour around the world. Chris met him at the hotel bar the night before and introduced the boy to his favorite drink—an Arnold Palmer. The other boy was about fifty yards ahead when Chris fell, and he only heard a short yell before there was silence. Authorities questioned the boy with fervor, suspecting foul play, but the motive was never there, and they eventually let the devastated young man leave the country.

When Mike and Lisa received the call, Mike crumbled in a heap on the ground. Lisa could see the news in his eyes. She began screaming at the air for answers and details. Few would come, but not for lack of trying. They both flew to Thailand and spent a week searching for more information, but to no avail. They even flew to Spain where they met up with the young American boy, who only brought them condolences and more sadness—but nothing by way of answers.

As was her habit, Lisa continued to check on Chris' blog. She had an unfounded hope that Chris might still be alive and missing, but mostly she checked back out of habit and disbelief. *He was here just a week ago*, she thought.

A day after Mike and Lisa landed back in the states, Lisa found herself stunned sitting in front of her computer. A brand new post was staring back at her. Fresh words glowed on her computer display. Could it be? New words from her son? There it was, calling out for her.

"Freedom is seldom found by beating someone to the ground, telling them how everything is gonna be now."
June 2nd

I can't quite describe the frustration I encounter when faced with evangelical religious-types. I find their position on the way the world works considerably obtuse. The other day I was approached by a middle aged Brit spending time "saving the world" in Thailand. He wore a fake smile on his face and patronized me by calling me brother when he approached.

"How are you today, brother. Have you accepted Jesus into your heart?" It was clear that there was tremendous pain behind his eyes. Pain he was hiding and running from. The smile couldn't hide the pain. And he called me brother...

I wouldn't be bothered by this mangled toothed gentleman's reference to me as his brother, if it felt real. I can accept, or at least respect, the thought that we're all experiencing the same joys and pains in this life, and we are all interconnected on this crazy journey, but the "brother" just seemed forced. Oddly, the O'Jays rang in my head as I smiled back at him—*How can you call me brother when you ain't even searching for the truth?* What he meant to say, in my estimation, was, "Hello there. Do you believe the same thing as I? If you do, we are brothers. If you don't, then I cannot accept you as my brother, other than insofar as you may some day change to be more like me and then we can be brothers." It's laughable to me.

Despite my better judgment, I entertained this man's approach on this particular day. As we talked more, he began to speak quite horribly about homosexuality, adulterers and an entire slate of things. At one point, I became so embarrassed by what he was saying that I began looking over my shoulder for fear of being directly associated with this man. I asked him why he was convinced homosexuality was a sin, to which he provided oft quoted and incorrectly cited passages of scripture clearly taken out of context. Despite "judge lest you be judge" and "let he without sin throw the first stone," this man and so many like him seemed to hide behind the farce that they are not the ones judging, God is. They are simply the messengers of God's judgment. And so we hate, fight, spit, spew bigotry, murder, torture...all in the name of something good and holy. Every religion. Every era. I don't see an end in sight.

It's not the idea that he believes a man died for him and all of humanity over 2,000 years ago, and he finds peace and solace in this. I have no issue with that. Religion and faith are full of abnormalities and paradoxes. Faith is to be respected, maybe the most respected. It's the idea, though, that I need to conform to see the world the way he sees it in order to really live life. I can't wrap my head around how small-minded this is. It's the idea that he needs to convince me to "convert" to his way of life, and causing pain and suffering is acceptable for this end. He needs to beat it into me. I prefer to believe in a world that is much bigger than one size fits all. I simply can't see how violence and death in an effort to push the agenda of any particular religion, is the answer. There's no truth in that. If there is a God, if there are merits of this man's crucifixion, may the world realize this and by some mercy, let us stop fighting.

Lisa stared blankly. The harsh white light from the internet page glared on her face. *There's a new post*, she thought, confused with hope. She sat not comprehending a single word she had just read. Then, without notice, the tears poured out. She began to sob uncontrollably. She reached out and touched the screen. She reached out in agony, in attempt to touch her son before her. She felt the warm buzzing screen, the warmth of the display.

....

Two days later, Lisa found another post. Well, in actuality, Mike discovered the new post this time. When Lisa first described their son's new blog, Mike immediately dismissed it as grief-filled ramblings. It was a day later before he even checked back to the website. In his mind, he thought that if he visited the site with Lisa, they would find it unchanged from weeks ago, and her odd infatuation with a fake new post would be forced to subside. What he found, instead, he was not expecting. He was surprised to find she was right.

"See," Lisa said without being smug.

"Oh my god," was all Mike could muster. He kissed his wife and began to read through tear-filled eyes. He barely understood a single word on the screen before him. Thoughts of his son now rushed through his mind. Tears one at a time ran down his cheek, slowly but consistently. When he finished, he kissed his wife again and walked to the front porch of their old Victorian home. He spent the rest of the night there staring at the towering oak tree in their front yard. He loved this oak. Its branches alone were the size of tree trunks. The neighborhood grew around it over the years, but the oak always stood tall. Soon, within the next year, Mike would watch his beloved oak tumble to the ground, but now he sat thinking about his son, and aching from how much he missed him.

The next day, he checked back to re-read the mysterious post. To his surprise, another post had already refreshed on Chris' website. The words radiated off the computer screen to Mike, simple and succinct.

"The only line that is true, is the line that you're from."
June 4th

Life oftentimes gets in the way of living. We take painstaking effort to make a living only to forget about our life. We get so caught up in the details of our life only to disregard the enjoyment we get in actually living it. Remember to enjoy your day today. Tell your friends you love them. Hug your family. Clichés are obnoxious and démodé, but they become clichés for a reason and it's not because they're untrue. Tell your loved ones you love them today. You don't know when you'll be afforded the opportunity again.

For me, I love my family. I hold onto them tightly. Keep being a model of a man, Dad. I emulate you.

Mom—You gave birth to me. You raised me.
You loved me. You put up with my antics and
constant questioning of authority, ever the idealistic juvenile. Yet you always loved me. Each
day I behold the love you have for me. Why you
love me so much, I'll never know, but I love you
for it more than you know.

Mike was honored by his son's simple words.
He found himself smiling without sorrow, not because he wasn't sad, but because he was happy that
he raised such a well-adjusted boy. *Through no doing
of my own*, Mike thought.

Lisa and Mike began checking the site regularly.
Since Chris' apparent death, they had found themselves drifting away from each other. They found
that the blog was the only thing that kept them
connected, and they found they both dealt with
sorrow completely different from the other. Mike
focused his pain and sadness into his work. He
wanted to remember his son and push on each day
with the fervor that Chris would. He loved the gift
the new blog posts brought him, but he didn't believe for a moment that his son might not be dead.
Lisa, though, had a much harder time. She fixated
on a number of different conspiracy theories—the
other American boy murdered Chris, or the other

boy didn't mean to but still caused it, or the Thai government caused it and covered a mistake of one of their own, or, one she seemed to become more fond of with each passing day, Chris wasn't actually dead. Lisa never spoke these out loud at first, but over time she began to voice them.

At one point, Lisa asked her husband point blank, "Do you think Chris is still alive?"

Mike sighed; the pain of such an idea frustrated him. He wanted to move on, not to forget Chris, but to keep living. "No, honey. Chris died."

"Yea..." Lisa said as her voice trailed off. She stared across the kitchen table not looking at Mike, not looking at anything at all. She stared into nothing. "It's odd they never found his body though, right? It makes you think maybe he really isn't dead."

"No, Lisa. It doesn't make me think that at all."

"Well, why not? Not even a little bit? It's possible that Chris is still alive. Maybe it's a small possibility, but it's possible."

"No, it's not," Mike said matter-of-factly. He wasn't responding coldly to his wife; he simply struggled to even entertain the idea. "He's not alive, Lisa. He's not mysteriously missing but still posting on his small blog somewhere. Why in the world would he do that? I know finding his body would bring some sort of closure, but we don't need closure through seeing his body. We have the memories of Chris, the laughter he brought us, the frustration he caused always challenging common perceptions, the excitement he gave us. We'll always have that from our son, and the peace of knowing that he was our son. We raised him. But he's gone, Lisa."

"Well I still have hope, however small it may be. I don't get how you can let him go so quickly."

"I haven't let him go. I lay awake at night with an empty hole left in my life, in my soul. But I don't want to forget the rest of my life. I want to put the pain I feel into each day. I'm trying to keep living, but I haven't forgotten."

"It feels like you might have. I wish I could live my life, but I just can't. I carried him for nine months, gave birth to him, breastfed him, loved him. I simply can't move on, especially if there's a chance he might still be alive."

"I love him too, but there's not a chance he's still alive. It pains me to say it, but there's not."

"Think what you want. There's a chance." Lisa's voice was distant now. "Why do you think there's been two more blogs? It makes no sense."

These words trailed off looking for a home but drifting through the air without finding one. She slowly slipped from her chair and went to the computer in the next room. She found herself reading and re-reading Chris' old posts every day. Lisa longed for another connection with him. She wanted a new post to be there. She was granted that gift when the webpage loaded. *See,* Lisa thought to herself, *there's a chance.*

I can see straight down your crooked teeth. You feel so dumb, mouth open large. You've got exactly what I'm drinking for.

June 15th

He came out of nowhere and stunned me. A short statured Indian man popped out of a small alleyway the other day. He looked ragged, tired, hot. "Watah," he exclaimed.

"Whoa. Excuse me?" I responded, surprised as much by the fact that he was speaking to me in English on the streets of Thailand as I was by his quick approach. The majority of the English I've spoken over the last few weeks has been either in my head or with a lot of gestures and pointing. I've heard even less spoken to me.

"Can I have some of your watah?" he clarified in very good English.

I looked down and noticed the Nalgene bottle hanging from a carabiner on my backpack. "Sure, I guess so."

So I shared with him some water. He opened his hands out to me, as if suggesting I pour the water into his cupped fingers. I insisted he drink directly from the bottle. There's something about traveling and living in dingy hostels that changes your disposition to grimy strangers, I guess. I've found that people are more willing to assist with someone else's homeless people. For some reason, the man struggling on the street in your own hometown is easy to ignore, but find a man on the street halfway across the world, and we all become bleeding hearts. I found myself reacting the same way. Maybe I assume the homeless man in my own city has been afforded the same opportunities and options in life that I've had, but I don't know what the man in a foreign land has been afforded. I'm not sure what it is. It's a silly way to think, whatever it is, but I digress. Back to the man on the street in Thailand.

The man drank the smallest sip of my water, to which I encouraged him to drink more. He clearly needed it more than I. After a long gulp, he looked into my eyes and frowned. I patiently waited for him to say "Thank you," but he didn't speak a word. Finally, surprised that my supposed kindness was not being recognized or appreciated, I shrugged and said, "You're welcome."

I saw a smile creep across his face. He looked up at the sky, then to the ground at his feet, then directly into my eyes again and said in his Indian accent, "For what? For sharing with me what you have plenty and I have none? I'll notify the authorities to throw you a parade."

Once again, I stared at the man in amazement. It seems that's all this man caused me to do—be stunned. He popped out of nowhere and startled me. He acted as if I would pour water into his fingers. He took the smallest sip possible for his first drink. Then after drinking nearly half the bottle, he mocked my desire for thanks. I was stunned. He didn't say another word to me. He nodded politely and turned back down the alley.

I stood for a moment unable to move. What just happened? I slowly walked away pondering the encounter in disbelief. It's stuck with me since. I can't seem to shake it for some reason. I would typically chalk the encounter up to him being rude and disgruntled. He wasn't though. He was polite and unfailing. I, on the other hand, was startled and entitled. And, at that point, out of water.

Lisa smiled at the screen. "See," she mumbled again to Mike, knowing full well that he couldn't hear her.

Maybe it was the timing of the post, right after the argument with Mike about whether there was a chance Chris could still be alive. Maybe it was her inability to accept what everyone else was telling her. Whatever it was, Lisa became fixated on the possibility of Chris still being alive.

She began by calling the local police. An officer was sent to the house of the frantic woman explaining how her dead son might still be alive. The kind officer took notes about the death of their son in Thailand, but it was clear he'd drawn the short straw among all the officers down at the station. Lisa didn't seem to notice, though, and pointed out blog post after blog post.

"I'm not saying he's clearly alive," Lisa acknowledged. "I'm just saying it's a little odd isn't it?"

"Maybe his account was hacked, ma'am," the officer responded kindly. "Or maybe Chris has friends that wrote with him, and they are still writing. Maybe it's their way of coping."

"Chris would never let anyone write for him. It just doesn't make sense. Maybe he's kidnapped somewhere, but still has access to the blog."

The officer nodded politely, wanting to point out that if her son was kidnapped but still posting blogs, it would probably make more sense for him to be posting messages of distress or cries for help. He opted to keep it to himself, realizing that reason had left this discussion long ago.

At one point, Mike looked at the officer as if to say, "Thanks for humoring us." Lisa caught the glance and felt completely betrayed.

"Thanks a lot," Lisa said and marched off upstairs. Both Mike and the officer stared at each other briefly, unclear what words should be exchanged next. After the pause, they exchanged niceties and shook hands.

"Tell your wife we'll be in touch if anything comes up."

"Thanks so much for your time," Mike replied as he closed the door behind the police officer.

....

The next month was more of the same for Lisa. She contacted foreign authorities, she posted on missing children websites, and she talked to anyone who would listen. She found herself spending hour after hour on the internet, chatting with support groups and researching missing children options. She particularly was drawn to Hope More, a support network for families with missing or exploited children. The group was made up of individuals, like Lisa, who had been forced to live the nightmare that no parent wants to face. Lisa found parents who had experienced a similar pain and who were coping with the trauma. "You're not alone. We're here to help you!" That was Hope More's motto. Lisa found purpose searching on these sites, but she found no comfort. They told her she was not alone, but it certainly felt like she was.

Mike had originally thought this would end, but it only seemed to get worse. Lisa would wade through each day in a daze. She wouldn't sleep at night. On nights when Mike couldn't sleep, he would wander downstairs to spend some time on the front porch. He would always find Lisa in the same place, parked in front of the computer.

"I'm searching for answers," she would tell him hollowly.

But Mike knew the haunting reality: there weren't answers. Their son had tragically died far before his time. There was pain, anger, sadness, despair, hatred, regrets, and on and on, but there were no answers. He believed Lisa knew this too, yet there she sat for hours every night. Like a drug addict needing a fix, Lisa would search internet page after internet page chatting with parents whose children were missing. She believed relief would come from her time spent online, but she was only left with the agony of her son being gone.

Sometimes, when Mike would wander downstairs in the middle of the night, he would try to comfort her. He would find Lisa staring into the haze of the pixelated display. The harsh white light would illuminate her face amidst the darkness of the room around her. Mike tried talking to her; he tried sitting there with her; he tried making her food; he tried rubbing her shoulders; he even one time brought a pillow and blanket downstairs and slept on the ground next to her. Signs of solidarity, he'd hoped. None of it seemed to break through the cloud of sadness that enveloped Lisa.

During one of his attempts to reach out, Mike was unable to sleep and was headed for the front porch. As he wandered to the kitchen to first make a cup of tea, he noticed Lisa sitting in her usual late night perch. He made two cups of tea and set the second next to the keyboard in front of her. Mike reached to rub her shoulders, which were tense and strained from weeks of hovering over the computer. His touch startled Lisa, as if awakening her from thoughts of a distant world. Her body shied away from Mike's approach. Without looking at him, Lisa got up from her chair and slowly shuffled away.

Mike fell into the chair defeated. Before him were two internet windows. One was riddled with searches of missing children support groups and tips on convincing authorities to do more to search for a missing children. Mike sighed despairingly when he saw the webpages.

When will it end? Mike thought to himself.

The other page was Chris' blog site. A new post haunted the screen.

> *"And the world is so much meaner when your heart is hard."*

July 7th

I've recently been pondering how much I fight myself. I want to love and share love. There's so much fighting and hate in this world and I don't want to be a part of it, but this is difficult in practice. I find myself constantly fighting against loving. A man on the bus slighted me yesterday, and I stewed over the incident. The lady at the gas station was rude, and I couldn't just let it go. Why do I have such a hard time letting go? If I could offer up my time and thoughts to more important matters, if I could focus my energy on the things I care about, if I could commend my spirit to love, wouldn't I be much more peaceful? Wouldn't the elusive and mysterious happiness be much closer? It's interesting to ponder at least.

Mike found himself not thinking much about Chris' latest post at all. He couldn't shake the constant sinking feeling that he was losing his wife. He decided he needed to take action. As he sipped his cooling tea, he decided Lisa's fixations on conspiracy theories and the possibility that Chris may still be alive had to end. They were keeping her from moving on with her own life. They were driving the two of them apart.

The next morning, he began searching for a logical explanation for why the blogs were being posted. He started searching on the internet for some explanation. He also began to more directly and more often suggest to Lisa that she should begin to accept that Chris was dead. When his own searches proved fruitless and Lisa's obsession continued, Mike called a few of Chris' friends to see if they had any information. They all expressed their condolences and sadness, but none of them had any information on Chris' blog and why there were new posts.

After a number of weeks of his own efforts, he decided to commission one of the IT guys at his office to help, fully expecting they would track the IP address that the posts came from to one of Chris' friends. A week later, after a little digging, Mike's coworker came to him with some information.

"Live long after dot com," the IT specialist said as he laid a post-it on Mike's desk.

Mike picked it up and held it in his hand as his office mate continued. "Apparently, it's a website that will continue to post blogs for you after you've died. Actually, they'll do more than just post blogs. They'll send letters, packages, money, secrets, a whole variety of options, each for a different fee. I guess it's a way to remain relevant after your death or to patch up past regrets from beyond the grave. A little eerie if you ask me.

"The blogging option seems simple enough by the description on their website. Upload as many prewritten blogs as you'd like, and they'll post them according to the schedule you laid out after they've received word of your death. They have algorithms constantly scrolling news sites and the internet for death notices on their clients. Chris' posts are coming from their IP address."

As a range of emotions flooded Mike's thoughts, his coworker continued. "I called them up, but they wouldn't give any information. 'Confidential,' they kept telling me. They're located in India, but apparently have clients from all over the world."

He paused. "I'm sorry, Mike."

....

The weeks that followed Mike's discovery were when everything finally drifted apart. Mike left work early that day and found Lisa at the computer again. She was reading a new blog written by her deceased son. She had a sad yet wistful look in her eyes. Mike crouched down next to her and grabbed her hands in his.

"Honey, I found out where the new posts are coming from."

Mike then went on to explain what he learned from his coworker. He had called the company himself later in the day and was able to guilt the poor customer service rep on the other side to give him more information. Chris had contacted them via email over a year ago and paid the minimum fee for ten blog posts. The representative said she could lose her job for sharing the information. Mike thanked her, telling her that she was giving peace to the parents of a dead son.

Lisa's eyes were hollow by the time Mike finished. The wistful glint was gone. The sadness had darkened. Her eyes were wet, but tears were not coming. She got up and walked upstairs past her husband.

Mike stood in front of the computer and then sank into the chair. Like a building that had just imploded, his knees broke, then his waist, then his shoulders, and finally his head sank into his hands. Mike wept uncontrollably in that chair. He had lost a son, and he knew he was losing a wife. The life he knew was crumbling before his eyes.

As Mike's head pounded from crying, he looked blankly at the computer. Chris' new post that Lisa had been reading was still on the screen.

*That you never saw the signs, that you never lost your
grip. Oh, come on now, that's such a childish claim. Now I
wear the brand of traitor. Don't it seem a bit absurd.*
August 15th

We can only be who we are. I'm not sure I believe that we have a calling, each of us. The closest I can come to buying this is that we are meant to be who we are. I guess you could say I am "called" to be me, no one else, no more and no less. The most forsaken are those who fail to know who they are, or even worse, know it but fail to be it. If we are true to ourselves, we should never feel forsaken by anyone; we should never feel inadequate. This concept is nothing new. Both Polonius and Theodor Geisel said it long before me, yet we have an incredibly difficult time doing it. Be yourself, no one else. That's all anyone can expect of you. That's all you should expect of yourself.

Mike found himself beginning to hate each of Chris' blog posts more and more. He missed his wife and found himself beginning to resent the fact that these blogs were driving them apart. In reality, each post was really only a conduit for the pain and distraction they both felt. Tragedy changes people, especially when that tragedy involves your own child.

As the days passed, Mike could see Lisa drifting away with every passing moment. There seemed to be nothing he could say that allowed them to reconnect. The distance between them was becoming insurmountable.

"How can you appear so calm?" Lisa asked one Sunday morning as Mike was sitting at the kitchen table with his coffee and reading the newspaper. Her question was posed with a sense of desperate longing, a need to understand how Mike did it, as if he had some undisclosed secret. There wasn't a hint of disdain or judgment in her voice.

"Lisa, I've learned a lot of things through this terrible experience. One of those things is that everyone handles sorrow differently. Everyone mourns in his own way. What you see as calm is just me grasping for a semblance of normalcy."

Lisa didn't hear him. She continued with another question. "Why did you have to show me that website? Why did you have to confirm Chris' death? Out of all people, why did it have to be you that finished it?"

Mike sighed. Taking a long drink of his coffee, he thought for a minute. "I've seen you struggling, honey. I've seen you flailing in despair. I wanted us to move on together. I wanted us to meet this head on together."

"I don't want to just move on, Mike. I can't move on."

Lisa grabbed the whistling teapot from the stove and filled her mug. "You just said it yourself—we each mourn differently. Why couldn't you let me mourn? Why couldn't you let me hold on to the hope of our son being alive? You took him from me again."

....

Lisa squeezed Mike's hand as he bent over to light the candle sitting at the base of the grave. The wind momentarily died down as if to assist.

"We raised a good son," Lisa whispered.

"You were a good mother," he replied. "You cared for him like a saint. You gave him everything."

Lisa smiled as if to acknowledge her appreciation of the kind words. Her thoughts wandered, and her eyes drifted across the graves that stretched out before her. A family gathered in the distance. The family was quite large, maybe eight adults and another ten children or so. One of the adults was an elderly man. They each carried flowers and trinkets, one by one placing them on the ground. *A visit to their grandmother on the anniversary of her death*, Lisa thought.

"I'm sorry I had to leave," Lisa lamented.

"I know," Mike replied. "Me too."

They both stood peacefully holding the silence.

After what felt like years after Chris' death, but in actuality was less than five months, Lisa moved out. She could not take the reminders. Every room in the house, the cars they drove, the food they ate, and Mike, poor Mike, they all reminded her of Chris. She couldn't take it. The sorrow came in waves with each reminder. So with little fanfare, Lisa told Mike she would be moving out at the end of the week.

Mike half-heartedly protested. He didn't want her to leave. In fact, he longed for her to stay. He hoped they would be able to rebuild a life together, some fraction of the marriage they once had. He knew that this was no longer in the cards, though. Lisa had moved out of the house mentally months ago. While her physical absence would certainly add to the agony, he had been staring down the barrel of this reality for quite some time.

When Lisa left later that week, she kissed Mike goodbye on the cheek. Both of them fought back tears as they found themselves at a loss for words. What was there to say?

Lisa reached into her purse and handed him a folded sheet of paper. Mike instantly knew it was a new post from their son. Lisa liked to print out each entry.

"I love you," she said as Mike accepted the blog from her.

"I love you too," Mike replied.

Lisa collected her suitcase and turned to go out the front door. Mike sat in disbelief on the couch at the front of the house. He was numb from the agony of it all. He unfolded the paper in his hands. A blog from Chris hadn't appeared in quite a while.

"Please don't you leave me, I feel so useless down here with no one to love though I've looked everywhere."
October 24th

Everyone wants to love and be loved. We often look for the love of others to save us. This is not a new concept. I don't purport to be providing deep insight into the world. It has been written about since the time of the ancient thinkers.

Sophocles knew that love is the only freedom from the weight and pain of life.

While it may not be a new concept, it is quite an astounding one, both in its simplicity and in its difficulty to grasp in our every day lives. Each of us yearns to love and be loved, yet we constantly push that love away when it approaches. We're afraid to be vulnerable. We are our own persecutors. We are crushed only by the mountains we create. Our need for love is our collective search as humans, it is common to us all. Our constant failure to accept love is because of our own arrogance, addictions, pride, and fear; this failure is the fastening of our hands and feet to the fate of our misery. Maybe Sophocles was right thousands of years ago, we are the sole cause of our adversities.

Mike felt the cynicism building up inside of him. His immediate thought was that his son, his dead son, was naïve. He couldn't fight the immediate reproach he felt. It washed over him like dirty dishwater. His wife whom he loved dearly had just walked out of his life because the son he missed and loved deeply was no longer with them; because he knew deep down that she thought he didn't love his son enough because of the way Mike mourned his death. Now he felt as if his son were judging him from beyond the grave. Mike understood the absurdity of the feelings that were rushing over him, but that's the irony of feelings. They tend to control much of what a man does, but they are rooted in emotional reaction, not logic.

Yet Mike's feelings, which were once sadness and loneliness before his wife walked out their front door, were now anger. After that day, Mike began covering his feelings of loneliness with anger. It didn't take long at that point for Mike to cover his feelings of anger with alcohol. He would go to the cupboard for the whiskey and drink until he couldn't feel a thing. Love, sadness, loneliness, anger, they were gone, awash in a sea of whiskey.

Things went on like that for two months. Mike kept thinking Lisa would return. He would arrive home from work every day expecting to see her on the front porch, but she would never be there. He would turn on the television for company and with every creak of the wind outside or slam of a car door down the street, Mike's ears would perk up in anticipation. Lisa would never arrive, but the alcohol would. He was numb, and the alcohol allowed him to actually feel; at least that's what he convinced himself.

In actuality, he was too scared to feel anything anymore, so he ran to the bottle to hide. It was a safe and comfortable place. Lisa sat across town in a similar fashion, not running to alcohol, but she hid in a host of other things. She continued to "investigate" her son's death. She made slideshow montages of her son's life. She drowned in her sorrows and lost touch with most everyone near and dear to her. She fell into a cloistered routine that alienated her from everyone she ever knew. No one could understand her pain and her sadness, so she stewed alone amidst sepia photographs. In the end, both Mike and Lisa were grasping for lifelines wherever they could find them.

They would speak occasionally over the phone, but as the days wore on Lisa became more distant and Mike began to give up hope that they could return to any normal life together. They met up for coffee once. It was clear to Mike that Lisa was simply checking up on him to make sure he still cared about Chris, and it was clear to Lisa that Mike was just wondering when she would move on and they would get back together. The conversation stagnated quickly as they just spoke about the weather and the latest news.

Not long after that, Mike cut back on his drinking, slowly at first until eventually he cut booze out completely. His had been a two-month bender on the train tracks of a functioning alcoholic. Mike missed drowning his sorrows at first, but soon he felt better. He found solace in cold winter walks and cups of tea by the fireside. Moving on from his son was never something he'd wanted, but it was something he was callously forced to face. In reality, he didn't move on, he simply kept moving. He found he would sink into a desolate despair if he stopped, or he would lean heavily on alcohol, so he just kept moving. It wasn't so much that he moved on from his son, as it was that he was just forced to continue. He was forced to face a similar reality in his marriage.

It was only a few days after cutting his drinking that he found Chris' latest blog. Mike had stopped checking back to the blog on a daily basis. He found this one had been posted for three days already.

> *"If my savior comes, will you let him know I've gone away for to save my soul."*

December 15th

I watched a young woman the other day who was completely distraught over her lost keys. She was riffling through her purse and frantically checking her pockets. As I sat at a café across the street, I could hear her mumbling things to herself not so quietly. *How can you be so stupid? What the hell is wrong with you? You ALWAYS do this? You're going to be late; serves you right.* I smirked as I watched her because I could see what she couldn't.

The keys, the ones for which she had been frantically searching, were sitting right in front of her just on the other side of the curb. I quickly realized that as she was overwrought on the sidewalk, she was unable to see the keys, which were gently hidden wedged up against the curb. I walked across the street and handed her the keys.

Maybe this is how we all live our lives. Maybe what we need is right in front of us, if we'll only take a moment to actually look. Like Peter Leavitt's Rule of 48, maybe it's not just scientists that are blind; maybe we're all blind. What if the happiness we've always wanted, our own personal heaven in this cruel world, is actually all around us? What if our bliss, our utopia as a society, is in fact right here in front of us, pent up in the subtleties of life? Maybe we just have to peek over the edge of that curb.

Mike sat momentarily before grabbing his jacket and winter hat. He waded out into the cold winter air. He could see his breath before him. The night was peaceful with the thinnest layer of snow blanketing the earth. Soon the snow would accumulate into larger snow banks, and the cold nights would drag on well into the new year, but for now, on this night, there was only a thin cover of fresh snow.

Mike wandered the streets longer than normal for how cold it was. He found the temperature stimulating. It acted as a cardiac shock to remind him that despite the pain, he was still alive; he could still feel through the fog of sorrow. There wasn't another soul out that night as Mike wandered the neighborhoods. The stillness seemed to call him in deeper as he walked. It was over an hour before Mike found himself back at his front door staring at the massive oak tree in their front yard, exhausted, quiet, and alone.

....

Mike knelt at the gravesite and kissed his fingers. The sun continued to shine brightly. It had been a year since Chris' passing. It had felt like a lifetime. He placed two fingers on the stone and whispered, "I love you."

As he rose to his feet, Lisa handed him the handkerchief she was holding. Mike wiped his tears away and thanked her.

"You think that's it?" Lisa asked, putting the handkerchief back into her purse.

"What's it?"

"Do you think this is the last one?" She pulled the folded blog back out of her purse.

Mike stood in silence for a minute, pondering as if Lisa had asked the meaning of life, or the meaning of death, for that matter.

"I'm afraid so," Mike finally replied. "It's finished. That's it. Isn't that what the last blog said?" Lisa unfolded the blog and read the last paragraph aloud again.

> So as I am stuck in traffic that's moving slower than I can walk, I realize that how I react to unforeseen problems, what I do each moment, what I even spend my time thinking about, they all greatly impact my character and my life's direction. Life's sim-

ple moments are not wasted and unimportant. They are the foundations that shape our lives. They are the formational moments, one added upon another. At least that's how I see things. But what do I know? One thing's for sure, I guess—it's finished. That's all I have to say. Thanks for reading.

She finished the final sentence with a question mark that wasn't on the paper as if to question whether Chris actually cared if anyone read his blog or to question whether she could accept they were finished.

"It is finished, isn't it?" she exhaled.

"It looks that way. I hope so at least. I don't know if I can handle any more. Constantly checking back to the website. The disappointment that comes when there's nothing new posted. Not to mention the range of emotions I face when reading those blogs."

Mike would have previously hesitated to say this, fearing that his words would hurt Lisa or that she would think it meant he didn't love their son. He no longer found himself able to worry about those things. He thought what he thought. He didn't want to read the esoteric words of his deceased son any longer.

"I'll miss them," was Lisa's response. "I found them cathartic."

"I know."

Mike reached over to give Lisa a hug. They embraced at their son's grave for a minute. Then, with all the love and sorrow and time the two of them had experienced together, Mike kissed her on the cheek.

"I'll always love you both."

He turned and walked back down the path from where he came. Lisa watched him follow the path as it curved out of sight behind a grove of trees.

"Me too."

Lisa sat down on the grass. She took her son's final blog and put it underneath the candle, which continued to burn protected from the wind and elements by its glass casing.

"Me too," she repeated.

THE DOMINANCE OF NURTURE

I t's hard to imagine there was a time when people thought differently, but they say it wasn't always this way. It's hard to believe. Like when people would throw witches into the water to see if they would float, or drain blood to rid the body of unseen demons, or manually drive automobiles down the highway at high speeds without automated assistance. It's hard to believe there was ever such a time, but there was. At least that's what they tell us.

When I was born, the science was still up for debate, not to mention the politics and ethics of it. "You just want to play God!" people would scream. "God decides, not you or I!"

People were just scared then. It seems silly now, but I guess it was a frightening reality for people who believed a higher power played a major role in the outcome of their lives, controlling every little decision and result like a puppet master. It doesn't seem odd to us at all now. The Greeks once believed Fate was a powerful force that controlled their lives, but in the 19th and 20th centuries everyone scoffed at this idea as a novelty of the times. "What an antiquated and uneducated belief system," they would say. But no one had a problem thinking of the important role their Western God played in their lives.

"He has a plan for me," they would say.

It seems a lot like fate in retrospect.

Dr. Arnold Cumberson was the scientist to first postulate the theory to the world—the Dominance of Nurture, as it came to be known. It fell mainly on deaf ears. A few science fiction magazines and blogs took notice and published his thoughts, but he didn't find a single credible scientific publication to carry his research until well after his death. Like a true scientist, however, he never seemed to waver. He simply continued to study the data before him.

Soon after his death, a few young scientists took notice of his work. In fact, it was brought to the mainstream consciousness purely by accident; although as we've come to learn through his research, even our very nature is merely happenstance. Except that they're not actually accidents at all, not in the way we once thought them to be.

Two young PhD students at a university out west were stoned one evening while reading sci-fi blogs. As they would often do, the two young men debated the far-fetched theories they found on their favorite blogs with the zeal only someone deep in a stoned haze can debate. When they stumbled upon a blog referencing the obscure studies of Dr. Cumberson, they became fixated on his ideas, so much so that they brought their thoughts to their professor the next day. And the rest is history.

Professor Mark Keaton is often widely misidentified as the discoverer of the Dominance of Nurture, but this is a misconception on the same scale as Christopher Columbus discovering America. Dr. Keaton helped popularize the theories. However, those of us who know the history know the real genius came from Dr. Cumberson.

When my son was born, my wife and I were well aware of the research. At the time of my birth, the subject was being hotly debated as Dr. Keaton tried to bring the theory to conventional acceptance. Thirty-some odd years later when my son was born, there was no longer a serious debate on whether the science was real; instead, the raging debate centered around intense disagreements on how to best approach child rearing. Right wing conservatives would shout to the rooftops that the left wing nut jobs were trying to remove god from the fabric of America. Left-wingers would shout back that the conservatives didn't love their children, and so their children were doomed for disaster. Of course, both sides were wrong, even in the parts they had right.

Like many geniuses, Dr. Cumberson died alone without recognition. In fact, he took his own life at the age of forty-nine. He left a note, for no one in particular, expressing the weight he felt as a result of his discovery, and the despair he encountered when no one took him seriously. By mere chance, his final note was saved. The coroner, finding a small slip of paper in the pants pocket of Dr. Cumberson's lifeless legs, kept the note. Years later, when we learned the magnitude of his discoveries, Dr. Cumberson's final note was preserved and kept in a museum somewhere—I'm not really sure where it's kept exactly, but I remember reading it once in a text book in school.

> *The untold truths of each act of man and the impact it has upon his life, his soul, his entire existence, have become too much to bear. I carry these burdens wherever I go. I am filled with them. My acts define me. It is impossible for me to loose myself of these burdens.*

That first day I held my son was as frightening and as joyful a moment as I've had in my entire life. My wife lay next to me, exhausted from pain and weariness. I simply stood with awed excitement. The doctors immediately ran their normal tests, sweeping our son out of our hands and into a nearby room. They tested for disease and the general health of the baby. The difference between these tests and those run a century ago on my grandparents, though, was that they weren't checking to see if God had given us a healthy baby. They were checking to see if my wife and I had successfully reared a healthy son in the womb.

When Dr. Cumberson's theories first began to be noticed, it seemed to thrust America into an outright panic. People were paralyzed with fear on how to best care for their children, unborn and otherwise. Some people said nothing should change at all in how we raise our children. "We cannot become overly concerned with every moment of every day!" they would shout.

Others argued that this was exactly what we should do. "With the knowledge we now have, we need to be mindful of every action we take. There are no innocuous moments in life. Every single moment and decision impacts our children exponentially."

When our son arrived, all manner of child-rearing theories still rang abundant. What became crystal clear, however, was that nature had very little to do with our make-up. Our personality, the very thing that gives us each individuality, isn't given to us by God or our genes. Dr. Cumberson's research put an end to the nature versus nurture debate. What he'd learned was that nature, in fact, had very little to do with any part of who we each are. What he taught us was that the characteristics that are passed on to us by our parents and our ancestry are very few indeed.

We now know that race, hair color, eye color, and general body type are impacted by who our parents are, but beyond that, the majority of our traits as individuals come from how we are nurtured. What type of food did your mother eat when she was pregnant with you? What music did your father play when you were in the womb? How late was your mother staying up during the second trimester? Was she sick with food poisoning late in the pregnancy? Did the doctor remove you from the birth canal a few seconds after you were prepared to take your first breath, causing fear and sudden panic in your newborn mind? Did your two-year old sibling land on your sternum when you were merely an infant? Did your father yell at you too loudly when you were a young boy? Did your mother force you to eat a food that was unappetizing and affected your brain chemistry as a young girl?

Whereas how much each action impacts our nature is still debated, what is no longer questioned is whether each and every action matters. The resounding answer is an unequivocal YES. You can imagine the panic every parent felt when the theories of Dr. Cumberson first gained traction. Every decision and every part of a child's environment impacts who they are? And not just a child, but throughout our entire lives, even as adults? The studies of food processing, alcohol intake, exercise, sleep, emotional communication, momentary reactions to stressful situations, television watching, the number of breaths per minute, the number of eye-blinks in a day, levels of human contact—all of it continues to be researched by scientists throughout the world to understand how to create the best version of our lives.

It was in this environment that I found myself first holding my son. At first, we believed we had a perfectly healthy child, but as he grew, it became apparent that this was not the case. Our boy struggled to focus. He couldn't concentrate on a task at hand, and when forced to, he seemed to understand more slowly than other children. While most kids learned to read somewhere in their third or fourth year, our son found himself still struggling to read when he was six.

"I hate this, Daddy," I remember him saying to me one evening as we practiced. "I'm stupid, aren't I?"

I grabbed my son and looked into his eyes. "You're not stupid. Don't ever let anyone tell you that."

But the guilt I had inside constantly haunted me. What did we do wrong? Why is he slower than other boys? Did I yell at him too much? Did I cook the wrong meal for my pregnant wife? While two hundred years ago I would have merely believed God had dealt my son a difficult hand, and we would learn to overcome it together, now I could no longer believe this. With the knowledge we now had, I knew that God hadn't dealt our boy a difficult hand; we had.

The judgment was almost as bad as the guilt. The looks from neighbors when we walked down the street were piercing. They would look at us in disdain. *Look at the negligent parents. How could they do that to their child?*

The doctors were no better. Every prescription came with the aside, "I wish the care had been taken sooner. We wouldn't need to be prescribing these medications."

It was all too much for my wife. She couldn't take the shame and the guilt. Shortly after our son's seventh birthday, she ended her pain. She had watched her boy struggle in tears one too many times. She had heard her son say, "I'm stupid," for the last time. I found her lying in our bed with a distant smile on her face. A note lay next to her.

My actions, son, have profoundly impacted your life, your soul, your entire existence. It has become too much to bear. I carry these burdens wherever I go. I am filled with them. I loose myself of these burdens.

The shock and depression hovered over me for years. I had become a cliché of the times—a single parent widowed because of the weight of nurture. There were too many of us. It had become all too commonplace. The discoveries of Dr. Cumberson were too much for many people to bear. They couldn't handle the responsibility, especially when it came to their own children. Knowing that every sadness their child experienced could somehow be linked directly back to them was too much for many parents to bear.

My boy and I soldiered on. Things didn't get easier for him either. When our neighbors would gaze at me with pity and scorn, I could see my boy feeling as if he were responsible. He heard the scoffs at school when he tried to read in front of the class. He saw the snickers when he worked on simple arithmetic. When he was ten, the city moved him into a school specifically quarantined for the slower children. He felt branded by the community.

It was as if the path of his life were dictated for him from the first day of conception—some people even argued it had been dictated even before conception—it was as if the physical and mental capabilities he had begun to display from the first day of life set him on his course for years. He didn't show intellectual rigor at the age of five, so he wasn't accepted to the best preschool. He was slow in understanding elementary concepts at the age of seven, so the teachers stopped calling on him in class. He wasn't allowed on sports teams or in summer camps, and finally he was moved out of his school.

At the age of thirteen, kids from the nearby elite junior high school pushed him around on his walk home and put him into a dumpster. I saw him running toward home a block away. I met him halfway down the block and hugged him.

"I can't do it anymore, Dad. I hate who I am. I don't want this anymore." Tears streamed down his face. I hugged him closely to my chest as visions of my wife flashed before me.

"Don't say that. You're an amazing boy."

"I'm stupid. Those kids are right; I'm a waste of space. Why didn't you do better, Dad? Why did you make me stupid?"

Every parent knows the heartbreak of raising a child; the moments when he is in need and you can do nothing about it. This was a hundred times worse. Not only could I do nothing about his pain, but I also felt entirely responsible for it.

I squeezed him tightly as he continued to cry. We crouched there on the front walk in a tear-filled embrace. I wanted to squeeze all of the pain right out of him. When his sobbing slowed and he began to catch his breath, I took him by the hand and walked up our front steps. He sat down on the stairs next to me.

"Son, you are the most resilient person I have ever known. You have a perseverance that none of those boys have. You have a fight in you that none of those boys can touch."

"I'm stupid, Dad."

"What is stupid?"

He looked at me confused, wiping the remnants of tears off his face.

"I'm serious. What does it mean to be stupid?" I pressed.

"Dad, everyone knows I'm stupid. You know I'm stupid. I'm too slow."

"So that's it? You're slow, and there's nothing we can do about it? "

He looked visibly angry that I was challenging him in this way. "It's done, Dad. Whatever you and Mom did or didn't do made me this way. There's no way to change that."

"You're absolutely right, Son. You are the way you are because of decisions your mother and I made, because of the doctors and your friends and your teachers at school and even those boys that picked on you today. But that's it? That's the end of the story? We should just pack up and close the book on our lives?"

I pulled him close to me and put my arms around him.

"What's your next decision going to be? How is it going to affect you? This isn't the end, Son. You're a fighter. You do it better than anyone I know. Stupidity isn't a condition, and you're not stupid.

"Yes, you struggle to learn as quickly as other children your age. You have difficulty with focusing and grasping the concepts your teachers are saying. So what? That's not the end of it. Fight, Son. Keep working. Your mother and I have had a tremendous impact on who you have become, for better and for worse, but the beauty of it all is that *you* are empowered to have the same impact on yourself. *You* control your own destiny. *You* decide."

He leaned into my chest, and I hugged him closer.

"Life isn't about controlling the things that happen to you, Son. Life is what you do with the things that happen to you."

My boy looked up at me and sighed. "I miss Mom, Dad."

"I know. I miss Mom too."

"Do you think we'll ever see her again, you know, like in an afterlife?"

"I don't know. What do you think?"

"I'm not sure, but I think I'd like to spend some more time thinking about it."

He hugged me and grabbed his book bag. As he walked to his room, he turned back to me. "Thanks, Dad. I love you."

"I love you too, Son. I love you too."

THE FOURTH SORROWFUL MYSTERY:

TWENTY-TWO

wenty-two steps. That's the distance from his front stoop to the pub around the corner. He should know. He's walked it a couple times a week for nearly three years. He didn't know how many steps it was, which in reality should not be surprising. How many people count their steps, even if they have walked the same path a thousand times? No one actually knows the number of steps it takes to get from one place to another. And neither did he. But it was twenty-two steps.

He sat staring longingly at the glass in front of him. The half-drunk beer almost glistened in the bar light. The red lucence from the fluorescent beer sign shimmered into his glass. An empty pint rested along the rail. To the right sat two fingers of scotch. He typically would settle for whatever came cheapest, but tonight he opted for something top shelf, or at least as top shelf as it comes for a neighborhood bar like this. He preferred bourbon on most nights, but tonight it was scotch. He took a long, slow sip.

He sat in his usual place, six stools in from the door. It was not really a special occasion, so there was no particular reason to be sipping a scotch. He felt extra depressed tonight, though. He had been fighting the depression for years. In reality, if he was in a moment of honesty, he would tell you that his emptiness was actually neither a depression nor something he fought. Rather, it was a lonely complacency that he welcomed with a sordid belief that it would bring him peace one day—not until it was time, however, as if he were condemned to carry his burden to its end.

A few nights every week he would end up here. Some nights called for one drink, and he was done;

other nights, three, maybe four. On the rare occasion he found himself unable to move homeward, he would imbibe with six. But it never went beyond that, and these occasions were, in fact, rare. He controlled his drinking as much as it controlled him, which almost made his relationship to alcohol worse. He sat, stool beneath him and drinks in hand, a calculated purgatory that no man would choose. But somehow he had.

Tonight he was on his third, including the scotch, and it would end there. He would leave the bartender twelve dollars for the drinks and three more for his effort, and he would walk home without saying more than a hello. Some days the two of them would chat about the weather or politics or sports. They would even discuss work at the docks occasionally, but it would never go beyond that. He never really discussed anything of consequence. Not on most nights, and not tonight. He stood up from his stool and wandered the twenty-two steps from door to door.

His thoughts drifted that night while he lay awake, but sound sleep did not arrive. It rarely ever did. When morning appeared, he would trudge to the docks to begin his day—loading heavy boxes was how he spent his days. It couldn't be considered his life, so to speak, because he was never fully present. He had never missed a day since he began the job six years ago, but he had never truly arrived either. He aimlessly worked, his mind never present in the docks, but his effort undeniably sustained. Forty crates to load, a half hour to complete the task. No time for a break. Rest would not come until his plight drew to a close. An intense suffering lay on his shoulders, but it lay there by his own doing.

....

The bartender sat out back smoking a cigarette. His day was about to begin. Soon his customers would enter for breakfast at the dingy bar, eating eggs and burnt bacon off of chipped, dirty plates. He served them with a smile.

"Ours is not to question why," he'd repeat the old marine adage that his father constantly incanted. "Ours is but to do or die."

He wished he could some days, but that desire was usually fleeting. He had a melancholic want for things to have been different, but he was comfortable with the reality that was his life. It was as if someone else had written a completely different script for him, but they were unable to deliver it. The heart-breaking thing, for him at least, was that he could see clear as day the other life hidden in that script. He knew what that life looked like.

An observer would never know the bartender held such deep-rooted pain. He wore kindness on his face that hid the sadness that lay beneath. He always smiled to every person that entered; without a hint of conceit, he served them.

The bartender removed the remaining chairs from the tops of the tables in the back of the bar and proceeded with his routine. Most of the pint glasses had been removed from the dishwasher the night before, but he removed the final glasses from the load that ran overnight. Along with them, he pulled out a dozen lowball glasses and another half dozen shot glasses. There was also a lone wine glass. This was not the kind of bar that often served wine, nor did it have separate glasses for red and white wine.

Each item he removed he inspected meticulously. With a clean cloth he rubbed out any smudges he saw, and due to the age of the dishwasher he owned, there were many. As he passed by the trashcan near the sink, he caught a strong whiff of soured beer. The bar always smelled of cheap beer and years of old cigarette smoke, but the trash can contained a stench even more pungent. He grabbed the half full bag and lugged it to to the dumpster out back. When he returned through the back door, he was immediately greeted by that familiar scent of stale beer again—the smell of his bar. This smell never ceased to make him cringe slightly a few times a day. It was a rather odd reaction for someone encountering this tincture at nearly every turn, but in reality he never cared for the odor of the beer he served, whether fresh or stale. It was never something he particularly enjoyed.

He walked patiently to each table and wiped it down with a rag soaked in warm, soapy water. He had each table cleaned the night before, but he did so again to be sure his customers had a clean surface off of which to eat. Then he restocked the napkins in each holder, made sure the salt and pepper shakers were full, and replaced the missing cocktail straws in the three containers along the bar. He cut limes and lemons but only after refilling the olives and cherries. He kept celery, carrots, pickles and even mushrooms underneath the bar for those who requested the bartender's special for their bloody mary. Otherwise, they would simply get salt, black pepper and olives to don their morning elixir. Finally, he checked each bottle of liquor and double-checked every keg. It was time to unlock the doors.

Sometimes a patron would be outside smoking a cigarette waiting for the doors to open at 10 A.M. Today there were three. It was cold this morning, and a fresh inch of white snow covered the sidewalks hiding the dirty, broken concrete beneath. A husband and wife tossed their butts at the sound of the lock clicking open. The freshly fallen snow immediately enveloped the still-lit ends of the cigarettes. The third gentleman wasn't quite finished smoking and took a few more drags out in the cold. The couple smiled at their familiar bartender and said good morning as they made their way to a table. He was over immediately with two yellow beers for them and a bartender's special for the gentleman still outside.

The older gentleman finished his cigarette and threw it in the direction of where the others lay. He came inside, and as he took his first sip of the bloody mary, he asked for a beer to accompany it.

"Rough night?" the bartender inquired.

The man smiled with a grunt and then, "Make the second a bloody beer."

The gentleman removed his cap to reveal his silver hair, which perfectly matched his winter beard. The bartender smiled back and greeted each new guest as he entered. "Have a seat anywhere, and I'll be right with you. Any drinks I can grab you to get your morning started?"

No menus were needed for his first table. They knew the breakfast options by heart. The new patrons, however, grabbed menus off the bar when they sat down.

As the morning dragged on, patrons came and went, some staying for four or five hours and some leaving as soon as they arrived. There were individuals that would down at least six beers before leaving to continue their days. Then there were those who didn't even have one drink.

Whatever your pleasure, the bartender thought.

He brought drinks and food throughout the morning and into the afternoon. He never once hurried, but he was always prompt with another drink or an extra napkin. Occasionally, he would sit outside with an old regular and have a smoke.

"How's the dog these days?"

"Did you get your truck fixed?"

"They say we're in for a long winter."

"Things going well for you?"

He was always there with a ready ear. His questions never pried into the lives of his patrons, but he never had to. They often opened up and dumped their pasts on him. Sometimes a drink or two was required, but the bartender was always there to listen. They were usually not looking for advice, so he rarely gave any. Sometimes, it was clear to him that some sort of counseling was necessary. In these instances, he let the patrons think that they had come up with the solution on their own. This always pleased them to no end. It wasn't an easy task, but years of experience helped him perfect his methods. He had been listening to people's problems for over eleven years now. Better educated people were paid a lot of money for the services he performed daily, but without a PhD he was simply a bartender.

....

The cold air at the docks was biting against his cheeks, but he didn't seem to care or even notice. He pulled his jacket tighter to his body. Finishing his lunch by himself, he stared out at the water. Some of the other workers threw a football around, while many others headed inside one of the storage warehouses to keep warm and play cards. He had played cards with them once and actually enjoyed himself, but he had never played again. They often invited him to play knowing full well he would decline. They hadn't asked him today, but that was because before anyone had a chance, he was already making his way toward the water. He slipped as he neared the wall along the waterfront, catching his balance on one of the stones that jutted out. He shuffled over the edge of the wall.

The water looked especially calm today despite a gray hazy mist enveloping the docks. He couldn't see more than two hundred yards off shore. A ship's mast in the distance looked fuzzy, as if in the background of a black and white charcoal drawing. It had little definition to it even though it was no more than four hundred feet away. Yet still the water looked calm. He thought he could lay afloat in its arms and drift off. He took a drag of the cigarette in between his forefingers. The smoke wafted from both his mouth and nose as he sighed.

His lunch hour was usually nowhere close to that. It rarely went longer than thirty minutes. Today, however, he couldn't pull himself away from staring out into the haze. He puffed on one cigarette after another as he allowed the haze of the day to envelope him. In the distance, the slate-colored water merged seamlessly with the ashen sky. Except for the occasional ship, the horizon held nothing but the powder gray of the early afternoon. He couldn't get enough of it. There was nothing to look at and nothing to do. He could simply be. The water and sky were at peace with how they indiscernibly merged into each other's drab existence, and he was content with their complacence.

Soon his contentment moved to melancholy. Things could have been different, and he knew this. It once again poured over him like it does so many times each day; like the misty haze enveloping the water, his was a heart breaking story that he suffered alone. Twelve years ago there were friends beside him, but most of them had long since moved on. And so he marched through each day because he still believed he needed to, he still believed he had to, he still believed there was a reason.

A wind began to drive off the water. He tried to move his body slightly to block some of the cold, but he slipped as he shifted and fell the four feet onto the rocks that lay between the wall and the water. Landing on his feet and catching his balance, his gaze hardly broke. The wind stirred up ripples of waves. He leaned back resting against the wall. As he continued to fixate on both the water and his past, he pulled another cigarette from his jacket and went back to work.

He connected the last clasp on the top of his jacket and moved toward his forklift. The snow had accumulated throughout the morning and into the afternoon. There were probably two and a half inches of white powder covering the black asphalt now, enough to make the afternoon's work more difficult. What did he care?

Turning toward his forklift, he lost his footing once again, this time on a hidden patch of ice underneath the snow. His feet slid out from underneath him, and he found himself staring up at the gray sky above.

....

Through the bar windows, the bartender could see the daylight slowly fading. These short winter days brought nighttime early and brought the after-work patrons even earlier. He knew they would be coming soon. He went through his routine cleaning the tables, restocking the coolers, and preparing for the night.

There was a time when he'd only worked nights, but when the previous owner had fallen on hard times and asked for his help financially, he had obliged with what little funds he could contribute to help the owner make ends meet. Through no grand plan, he had eventually become the sole owner of the bar. The owner before him fell further and further into debt and the bartender found himself taking a larger ownership share over time, until one day the previous owner stepped away altogether, and the bartender became a bar owner.

There was a time, years ago, that he would have become restless with the slow and monotonous pace of each day. The constant opening of the same door, cleaning of the same tables, filling of the same glasses would have ground him away like gears in a old car. But he found peace in the consistency of each day. He knew exactly what to expect. There were no surprises.

From time to time his wife would help out by straightening up or helping with liquor orders, but she usually chose to spend her time elsewhere on other things. He would always take a break in the early afternoon and let one of his other bartenders run the place. Sometimes he would break for an hour or two, spending time with his wife in the late afternoon. If it was nice, they would walk near the waterfront. On a day like today, they might play cards or watch a show. Many times, though, he wanted to be alone with his thoughts. It all depended on his mood. Today he only left for fifteen minutes. He went for a walk, but the cold wind whipping through the city streets quickly brought him back to the bar.

The snowfall had stopped for a short while, although the evening sky had now begun to fade to an ashen orange, and the bartender thought it might storm tonight. The fast-approaching darkness slowly moved across the bar as the sun set. The bartender traipsed through his pub flipping light switches and pulling chains that hung from the neon signs. Soon the bar glowed with that familiar haze.

....

A large shipment had arrived at the docks late in the day. Fearful of the slowly accumulating snow and not wanting the crates to sit outside overnight, the dock supervisor asked a few workers to stay late. He agreed to help out, not because he wanted the overtime, but simply because he had nothing else to do.

"Thanks," his supervisor said. "Take fifteen minutes, and then we'll knock these out before the snow gets too bad."

He found a small alcove between two of the warehouses and lit a cigarette. He watched the snow fall to the ground before him.

A few years after the accident, long before he ever worked the docks, a friend of his was able to get him to open up. His friend had always been a compassionate listener. Years of not being able to get a word in edgewise and just listening to his two older brothers had seemed to prepare his friend for the lifetime of counseling. He soon would enter the seminary and become a priest, but now the priest-to-be just wanted his dear friend to open up.

"You been sleeping alright?" his friend prodded.

"As much as I can," he sighed, which betrayed the fact that he felt the need to talk.

"That's great, right? It's been a while since you've slept much at all," his friend said trying to move the conversation forward.

"I guess. Sleep doesn't come normally anymore. Not the way it used to. It sort of just thrusts itself upon me, and I find myself waking up an hour later confused on where I am. I never ease into sleep. There's no process of going to bed like there used to be. No reading a book to doze off. It's abrupt, sudden. The sleep. Disruptive sleep. Intrusive thoughts."

His voice faded with those last words.

"Well at least you're sleeping."

"Yea, I guess. In the beginning I feared sleep. The daytime is easier. I can block out some of the thoughts. It's the sleep that's the worst. Transition-ing from sleep to wakefulness, and back again...I can't bear it. I relive it all over again. I relive it every day. The events play over in my mind."

His friend took a sip of beer, so he instinctively did the same before he continued.

"The thoughts. Intrusive thoughts. They come at all hours banging into my brain. I can't help but wonder what she was thinking. What was her last thought when the car struck her? Did she say anything? What did she pray for? What would she have been like today? So young..." he trailed.

He continued with a strained look in his eyes. "I thought about ending it a lot, you know," he said, not really asking a question. "I came close a few times. Pills. I just couldn't bring myself to do it. I don't know. I guess it seemed selfish."

"You can't think like that. You have to be easier on yourself. You need to find closure. Forgive yourself."

He took a long pause, staring through his friend. It was unclear if he had heard his friend's words at all. The silence was deafening.

"I don't think there's ever closure. I just...I don't think there is."

His voice rang hollow now. His friend's beer was empty. His own beer was nearly full. "There's a jagged hole in my heart. A hole has been torn in the middle of my soul. Maybe it will smooth over in time. Life will present moments. A wave of grace may present itself to smooth the jagged hole, but the hole will always remain. There's no closure. There's no filling the hole."

His friend searched for the words to console him. Despite shedding countless tears over the past forty months, he was overcome again. His friend cried and hugged him. He hugged his friend back without shedding a tear. There were no tears left for him to offer up.

It was the last time he had talked about it.

The crates moved quickly that evening, which was surprising because of the snow. It had continued to fall throughout the day. They weren't large flakes, but the constant dusting was now covering the asphalt entirely. The warehouse lot that began the day black was now a pure white. Tomorrow, when more than just two forklifts were running again, the freshly fallen snow would no longer hold on to its white purity. The forklifts would drag dirt and grease all around the lot. For now, however, while only a few of them worked into the evening, the snow graced the ground with whiteness.

The wind, on the other hand, continued to bite at their faces. The day had begun to wear on too long. As his lift carried the last crate to the platform, he looked into his coworkers' weary faces.

Their families, no doubt, awaited them at home. They would be sitting beside a gleaming fire sipping warm drinks in no time. They would hug their children close as they all dozed off.

His thoughts consumed him as he hopped out of his forklift to situate the final crate out of the elements. As he climbed down distracted, his forehead slammed hard onto the lip of the forklift roof, which was jagged from years of use. He reached for his head in pain only to find he had a gash just below his hairline. His fingers were black with grease and red from the blood that trickled out.

"You're exhausted," his supervisor yelled over to him as he jogged over with a towel. His supervisor motioned towards his face to indicate the cut, as if he hadn't noticed already.

"Nah," he responded, "just another day."

He grabbed the towel from his supervisor and slowly wiped his face. The towel felt cold and rough as he wiped the grease and sweat from under his eyes and the blood from his forehead. He sighed deeply as he tossed the towel back to his supervisor. A gust of wind caught it and blew it to the ground three feet away. The towel lay flat on the asphalt and snow.

"Hey, look at that," the supervisor chuckled. "It looks like a smiley face."

"Where?" asked one of the other coworkers. "I'm not seeing it."

The men remaining at the dock began to gather.

"It's right there." The supervisor laughed a weary laugh. "Turn your head this way. That towel has a bigger smile on it than I've ever seen from you," he ribbed.

"Yea, that thing's having more fun than you ever have," another coworker joked as he climbed out of his forklift and slapped him on the back.

"You guys are crazy," another jumped in. "There's just dirt and grease on it. And pretty soon, if you idiots don't get a move on, it'll be covered in snow too."

"Let me save you the trouble of the argument," he said as he picked his bloody towel off the ground and wiped his face again. More grease and blood smeared across the towel. "No more face, just dirt and grime."

The coworkers continued to chuckle as they closed down the warehouse for the night. They walked to their cars slowly. Their supervisor thanked all six of them for their extra work. He advised them all to pay close attention to the weather throughout the night because if it persisted at this rate, no matter how slowly the snow accumulated, they might not be working tomorrow. Most of them hemmed and hawed at those words, knowing full well that the docks hadn't been closed for a day in years. Forget the postman; dockworkers come to work every day. Always.

Each of them said his goodbyes, and he nodded solemnly to his coworkers as one of them slapped him again on the back. He removed one of his gloves to grab his keys from his pocket. The wind was impressively bitter as the dock floodlights flittered off the water's edge. His rundown pickup opened slowly with a subtle creak of the door. The metal truck felt the cold as much as he did. He turned the ignition three times before it finally started. Cold air blew at his face while he waited for the windshield to defrost. He closed his eyes and wrapped his arms around himself. A deep sigh leapt from chest. The air passed his lips, and immediately he could see his breath fill the space around him.

....

The bar was bustling. Every time the old wooden front door opened, the cold wind blew in another local. The bartender was always there with his warm gaze casting its glow upon their cold faces. Some of them broke away from the blustery weather to meet up with good friends. Others simply came to drink alone. Every one of them came to find solace in the company that lay within—communicative beings simply hoping that someone might hear.

The bartender had two waitresses managing the tables. The drinks flowed freely. After each glass was finished, the beer's owner looked fearfully towards the door and ordered one last drink before venturing into the cold night. The bartender slid a drink towards one of his regulars and grabbed a whiskey for a gentleman he hadn't seen before. The new face quickly put the whiskey back and ordered another. The bartender obliged.

As the bar was bustling within, the night continued to bring the bitter cold, chilling a man's head through to his skull. The two waitresses and the bartender hustled back and forth making sure everyone had their fill. All day frozen skeletons had burst through the door to take sanctuary inside the warmth of the bar, but they were slowly paying their tabs and venturing into the night.

As the crowd continued to thin, he entered the bar still in his dock clothes. His usual seat at the bar, six stools in, was taken, so he plunked down at the corner of the bar one seat further from the door.

"Beer?" the bartender greeted him.

He nodded his approval.

"Whiskey?" the bartender followed up.

"Please," he sighed.

"Another long day huh," the bartender stated. He filled up a pint of yellow beer and placed a shot glass before his regular. "It's freezing out there."

The bartender filled the shot glass up with well whiskey. The man took it and raising his glass to his ever-welcoming host, threw the shot back.

"Thanks."

"Not a problem. Let me know if you'd like another."

He gulped half of his first beer, washing away the cold, hard day at the docks.

"I would. One of each," he said pointing two fingers in front of him.

The bartender was prompt to fulfill his order, placing another shot and beer in front his guest. He quickly finished the rest of his first beer and handed the empty glass to the bartender. He turned to look around the pub and survey the scene. The bar that was once full of life was now much calmer. The dinner crowd had stayed well into the night, avoiding the cold as long as they could, but one by one they began to slip out the front door. It was nearly ten o'clock.

At a nearby table, a young woman and her boy-friend held hands. She fiddled with straw in her drink while the young man sipped on his Arnold Palmer. The girl beamed as the boy spoke. He was clearly trying his hardest to impress her. From the bar he watched with feeble amusement. The two young lovers exchanged an ardent glance and de-cided it was time to go. The boy pulled a twenty and then a one-dollar bill from his pocket and threw them onto the table, hoping he had accurate-ly calculated their tab. Then they slipped from the bar into the cold night with their arms linked around each other.

He smirked as he watched them leave. He re-membered being that young. It was so easy to live in the present when he was younger. There wasn't enough past to get in the way. He sipped his beer as his smile faded.

"Oh, to be young again, right?" the bartender caught him gazing.

He nodded in response to the bartender and threw back his whiskey.

"I knew when you walked in you'd be having a few tonight. Everything all right?"

"As all right as it ever is," he said.

"Can I get you another? One of each?"

"Please," he nodded.

The bartender brought the bottle of whiskey to the end of the bar.

"You're a good bartender," the man sighed. "I always feel welcome. You're a good man."

The two had spoke thousands of times over the years, but he had never intimated his appreciation of the bartender. If their conversation did ever go beyond a hello and a goodbye and a how-do-you-do in between, it typically drifted to city politics or sports or dock-gossip. He always expressed his gratitude for a new pour, but he never expressed his appreciation of the bartender as a man. Maybe it was the cold air. Maybe it was years of burdened shoulders from the weight of the past he carried. Whatever it was on this night, the bartender noticed an unguarded man sitting in front of him.

The tired bartender poured another whiskey in the shot glass in front of him and leaned up against the bar.

"Thanks," he smiled, hesitating whether to say anything further. He decided he would step through the door that his regular in front of him had barely cracked open. The bartender knew his job wasn't just to serve food and deliver drinks. No, his job, he understood, was to allow his patrons to unload their burdens.

A few more regulars finished their beers, paid their tabs and shouted their goodbyes to all.

"Stay safe out there," the bartender called out as he stood up. "And stay warm."

The bar had completely transformed in little more than an hour. What was once a packed sanctuary from the cold now held only a few regulars mostly keeping to themselves and staring at the TV behind the bar. The waitresses buzzed around, cleaning up tables and taking dishes to the kitchen.

"Why do you come in here every night?" the bartender asked.

He sipped his whiskey. "Where else would I go?" he shrugged.

"I've seen you a few times a week for years now. I know where you work and that you live nearby. I know your favorite drinks. I know without you even saying a word if it's going to be a one drink night or if you'll be staying a while. But I don't know a thing about you."

Another regular vacated his throne at the bar. "I'll get you next time," the man called to the bartender without paying for his drink. He tapped the bar twice with his knuckles and then zipped his jacket up tight. The cold air once again rushed in as another patron ventured out into the winter night.

The bartender returned his attention to the conversation at hand. "I know you don't want to share nothing about yourself, nothing of consequence anyway. I've known that from the first day you walked in here a few years ago. I've always respected that. But I also know that no man is an island. So why do you come in here every night?"

He shrugged his shoulders again and raised his pint glass to the last patron remaining at the bar. The patron obliged and raised his glass before downing its contents.

"Tha's all fer me gentlemen," the man slurred. He paid his bill, reassured the bartender that he was walking home and bundled up. Just like that, the bar had emptied.

The bartender began gathering empty glasses on the bar, stepping away from the conversation as if to give time to deliberate.

"Thanks for your work tonight, ladies," the bartender smiled at his servers as they began to help with the empty glasses at the bar. "I can take it from here. Get out of here before it gets any colder out there and the snow falls anymore."

"You sure?" one of them politely asked. Both waitresses hoped their boss wouldn't change his mind and ask them to stay.

"Yep," the bartender affirmed as both women breathed a silent sigh of relief. "You've done great work tonight as always."

They thanked him and slipped into the kitchen to head out the back.

"So what'll it be?" the bartender asked as he turned back to him.

He looked at the half shot of whiskey and nearly full pint of beer before him and knew the bartender wasn't asking what drink he wanted. He poured the second half of his whiskey into his mouth, letting it sit there a moment, burning his taste buds before he swallowed.

He raised his eyes up to the familiar face in front of him leaning on the bar. "I told you. Where else would I go?" he said quietly.

The bartender smiled kindly, understanding that he couldn't make the man say anything further. The silence would have been excruciating for a passing observer, but there was no one left to observe the two men, and the bartender was not afraid of silence. He had been faced with silence for years.

"I mean it," he continued, once again staring at the glass in front of him. "I have nowhere else to go."

The bartender grabbed the bottle of whiskey once more and filled his glass. "It wasn't always that way I assume?"

"No, of course not," he replied.

The bartender was beginning to wonder if he had read the man wrong. Years of being a barstool therapist had honed his skills in knowing when someone wanted to talk more than they were letting on. He had learned over the years to offer people a platform to talk if they wanted, but not to push them into the harsh stage lights of that platform. They had to take the opportunity themselves. The bartender was now second guessing himself.

"Did you see that young couple at that table over there earlier?" He nodded in the direction of where the young couple had left the bar arm-in-arm. The bartender nodded silently, not wanting to allow for any excuse for him to stop.

"They were something weren't they? So young, so wistful, without a care in world. We were that way once." He took long drink of beer as the words hung heavy in the warm air inside the bar that kept the cold night out.

The bartender knew there was a *we*. It didn't surprise him at all. There was always a *we*.

"I don't want to bore you tonight by talking about myself. My past is a sorry one. My story is full of sadness that I don't want to put on you."

"If you don't want to talk to me, that's fine," the bartender interjected, "but I assure you, you won't be putting any kind of sadness on me that I haven't already experienced in my own life, my friend."

"Trust me, my story isn't one you want to be bothered with. You have far too much to be happy about to be burdened with my story. It's not something you should have to carry."

"Try me," the bartender insisted.

He clutched his whiskey in his palm before he threw it back. The burn rushed from his tongue to his throat as he closed his eyes.

"I had a wife once, you know. We were the happiest couple on earth. I used to melt when she laughed." He rubbed his forehead as he spoke and stared through the bottles that sat behind the bar. A slight smile crept into the corner of his lips, but his eyes only reflected sadness.

"She had this way that she laughed at herself when she did something stupid. She would shrug in embarrassment. It was the most endearing laugh, so full of vulnerability and self-assurance all at once. It would always warm my heart."

The bartender had stopped wiping down the bar and pulled up a stool.

"We were just as naïve as that young couple. There wasn't anything that could separate us. 'Young love,' some people called it, but we knew it was more than that. We were together twelve years. Love weathers a lot of seasons in twelve years. We were inseparable."

He took a drink of his beer, eyes staring across the bar, but his mind was somewhere a long way off.

"We thought we couldn't have kids for the longest time, but almost ten years into our marriage, as we were considering whether we wanted to adopt or not, she got pregnant. It felt like we had been talking about adoption for years, but I'm not sure how long we discussed the possibility. We always found a reason not to begin the process. Then, without warning, she was pregnant. The doctors couldn't explain it. They chalked it up to an anomaly. They had told us there was a 99% chance we would never get pregnant, but there we were.

"We were absolutely ecstatic. While we cautiously tip-toed through the first trimester, we kept the exciting news to ourselves, fearful of miscarriage. I'm not sure if we even told our closest friends and family. But we sure did share our excitement together, especially my wife. She couldn't help but feel a huge weight had been lifted from her shoulders."

He paused a long time, not wanting to let the pleasant memories fade. He held on to that moment suspended in time. Finally, breaking the silence, he said, "Then it all changed."

The bartender was prepared for those words. Sad stories always contain those words. *Then it all changed.* He shifted on his stool, prepared to listen.

He drank the last of his beer and set the empty glass down.

"My wife had a doctor's appointment around the fourth month of the pregnancy. She was scheduled for an ultrasound, and we had decided to find out the sex of the baby. We were both planning on making the ultrasound, but an important work meeting came up, and I couldn't move it. We were so excited to find out the sex, though, that I encouraged her to go without me, and we would celebrate after.

"I raced home immediately after my meeting. I think we were planning to start telling friends and family that night. As I rushed home, my phone buzzed in my pocket. I pulled it out in excitement."

He motioned, reaching into his pocket and slowly looking at the phone, momentarily staring at his empty hand.

"'It's a girl!' it read. A picture of the ultrasound was there too.

"'A girl,' I thought. 'A girl!' I probably laughed out loud when I read that, 'Haha!' banging the top of the steering wheel a few times. I was going to be the father of a baby girl."

He then raised his hand again as if to hold his cell phone. His eyes fixated on his empty hand in front of him. The bartender stared at the hand as well.

"I looked again at the picture of the ultrasound. She was beautiful. My daughter looked amazing. I began texting my wife that I would be home soon. Then it happened. She came out of nowhere." The words drifted from his lips. His gaze never broke from his empty hand. His eyes began to well up.

"I hit her square on," his voice cracked. Tears welled up in his eyes. "I never even saw her. A little girl chasing her ball. She was nine, I think. Didn't even have a chance. Her mother rushed into the street after her, but there was nothing to be done. She held her daughter in her arms. I knew the moment I stepped out of my car... I stood in shock. The blood was everywhere. The mother's screams were horrific. There was nothing I could do. That girl's face still haunts my nights.

"Everything from that moment on was turmoil. Everything fell apart, but it didn't matter. That girl..."

His voice became distant and hollow. "The district attorney was consumed by the public's demands to stop texting and driving. My trial was fast tracked. I was charged and convicted of vehicular manslaughter, sentenced to two years in prison. I was locked up less than a month after it happened.

"I was out in eight months, but it didn't matter. Everything was gone already. That prison was nothing compared to the prison I've been in since. The stress was too much on my wife. She lost the baby two months after the trial. We lost our marriage not long after that. By the time I stepped out of that prison cell, my life was gone. I'll never forgive myself. I killed that little girl and my own daughter that day. She was twenty-two steps from her front door, that's what one of the papers had said. Twenty-two steps from safety. Just nine years old."

He looked up from his empty hand. He noticed the bartender for the first time since he began talking about that day. Tears were running down the bartender's cheeks.

"Ten," the bartender said quietly. "She had just turned ten." The bartender's eyes were fixed on the floor. "Her face was the most beautiful thing I had ever seen. And it still blesses my dreams every night."

He felt the blood rush from his head. The bar became blurry, and his gut exhaled as if it had been punched. He felt his throat tighten. His thoughts raced.

The bartender reached out his empty hand. It came at him, ominous and looming in front of his face as it approached. The tears continued to streak down the bartender's face as he placed his hand gently on his regular's cheek—this man he had seen thousands of times over the last few years.

"My life has been crushed with sadness too," the bartender said. "I had a daughter once, but she passed away. She lived a little longer than your baby girl whom you saw in the ultrasound that day. She passed away just after her tenth birthday. A tragic accident for everyone involved. She was chasing her kickball into the street when a car hit her. I was away on business. I hugged her goodbye that morning and told her I loved her. I had no idea it would be the final time."

The words echoed back and forth in his head.

Final time.

Final time.

Final time.

He couldn't make sense of what he was hearing. His thoughts continued to spiral around and around, unable to grab hold of a single one.

The bartender's hand took his shoulder as they both stood up, and the bartender led him step by step toward the front door, both men wiping tears.

"I have to close up now. My wife will be waiting for me and wondering where I am. I'm going to hold her especially close tonight. It's cold out there."

The bartender then reached his hand out and placed it once again on his patron's cheek. "You're welcome in my pub anytime, my friend. Maybe your life is a prison out there, but in here," he pointed at the bar behind him, "in here, you'll always be welcome. I hope to see you again tomorrow." The bartender gently patted his cheek twice and then opened the front door.

He stepped through the door in a daze. The snow was really coming down now. The street was covered in white. The light from the street lamps shone brightly off the snow-covered ground, illuminating the night. The wind was biting. The air was bitterly cold. He had never felt such a satisfying bitter cold in all his life. He breathed it in with each step home. Twenty-two times the cold air froze his lungs reminding him he was alive, one breath with each step. Twenty-two steps home.

BREATHE

Breathe.
One
Two
Three
Four
Beathe.
One
Two
Three
Four
Breathe.
One
Two
Three
Four
Breathe.
One
Two
Three

THE THIRD SORROWFUL MYSTERY:

EXPECT DRAGONS

aggot."

A leather-jacketed forty-something stared me down as he walked by me at a gas pump in Bozeman, Montana.

The word rang in my head like it has hundreds of times before, bouncing from the left hemisphere to the right hemisphere, from the prefrontal cortex to the temporal lobe, rattling around my brain without finding a home in my mind, but doing damage with its clattering in my skull nonetheless. This time was no different than any of the other times that I've been called that before.

I was no stranger to the hate-filled term. I've been hearing it since elementary school, even when I was trying to hide my scared and confused identity. Kids on a playground can be cruel, but when I was that young, my friends didn't realize the betrayal they were heaping onto my young soul. They simply mimicked what they saw their parents do. They didn't know any better because they weren't taught any better. In actuality, at that age it caused a young boy like me to be confused and afraid, but it hurt much more in later years when it was clear the betrayal was a conscious and deliberate decision.

The first time I can remember was second grade. We had just finished homeroom, and Mrs. Katzcross was dismissing us for lunch. I put my books neatly in my desk and went to grab my brown paper sack. My mom had packed me another bologna sandwich. It seemed to be a staple in my lunch those days—bologna, a slice of Kraft American cheese, and white bread. Mom always said she didn't add mayo or mustard because it ruins the delicious taste of the bologna, but I knew better.

Dad lost his job at the warehouse and cutbacks were made all throughout the Hinri home. Mayo and mustard weren't considered a necessity, so they were no longer in the fridge. The only condiment that did make the cut was ketchup, which you could find my sister and me putting on all sorts of odd things. Cheese sandwiches. Pasta. Chicken. Sometimes I'd even sneak some into our soup and stir it up.

As I walked to grab my lunch sack out of my backpack, I found myself wishing I had one of those little ketchup packets to squeeze onto my bologna sandwich. That's when I heard it for the first time.

"Are you a fag?" Tommy Connolly asked me.

I didn't know what to say. I didn't even know what he was asking me. What's a fag? What is he asking? My mind raced, as I stood confused.

Sweet Mrs. Katzcross, who always seemed to be there when trouble was a-brewing, quickly intervened.

"Tommy Connolly! We do NOT use that language in THIS classroom."

"But my dad asked the man checking us out at the grocery store the other da-"

"I don't care," my compassionate teacher interrupted. "We don't talk like that here. Now go, and don't let me catch you use that word again. Go!"

Then she looked at me with that kind smile that always seemed to melt my heart.

"Come here, James," she said as she grabbed my lunch sack from my backpack for me. "Mmm, bologna! Delicious!" she lied as she peered into the bag and then tousled my hair. I smiled as the confusion left, and things felt comfortable once again.

"James, this is going to be tough to understand. It certainly shouldn't be something an eight-year old should worry about, but I want you to listen closely."

Mrs. Katzcross sighed and looked me right in the eyes. "You'll learn that in this life, in this world, people think they need to label everything. They need everyone to fit into a nice little box, no matter how restrictive or damaging that box is. For them, everything is right or wrong, black or white. People are married or single, kings or poor, Republicans or Democrats. People will try to label you as a king, or dumb, or athletic, or any number of things. But I want you to remember this—you are not a label. You are not something that people can put into a box so they can better fit you into their worldview.

Never forget that, Okay? In this world, you're far more than any label."

I leaned in and hugged my teacher. "OK, I understand," I lied.

In truth, I had no idea what Mrs. Katzcross was telling me, but at that age it seemed like adults were never making much sense. Looking back on it now, though, I suspect she wasn't speaking to second-grade James Hinri. I think she knew I wouldn't understand what she was telling me then but hoped maybe teenage James Hinri or twenty-year old James Hinri would remember her words that day. As it turned out, I did.

Like a good teacher, Mrs. Katzcross called my mom that night to let her know about the incident. My mom was grateful for the call.

My father, on the other hand, already three beers in for the evening, took this as the opportunity to start training me how to be a man. This was the point, as far as I could remember, that my father began trying to fix me. From trying to correct my walk and how I held my hands to how I talked and who I hung out with. My father has tried to fix me my entire life. I tried for years to listen to my father—desperate attempts to please him. I wanted more than anything to hear him say,

"You did well, James." Those words never came. Instead, I only felt his shame.

My mom made sure to hug me closely and tuck me in that night. My second-grade self couldn't figure out the concern people had. First my teacher, now my mom? Why did they look so concerned? Kids pick up on everything, they just don't understand it all. I knew something was concerning to them. I just didn't know what. Turns out, they knew before I did. In second grade, labels meant very little to me. I believed we were all just who we are. I'm just me. Turns out—that's not the case in the real world. I guess Mrs. Katzcross and my mom knew before I did.

That day was the first time I was called that word. It was such an innocent exchange looking back at it twenty years later. Tommy Connolly had no idea what he was asking me, or how threatened and alone I would feel when I continued to hear the hate in that word in years to come. Faggot. He'd heard his dad say it, and now he was saying it himself.

Not all exchanges were that innocent.

This time, as the man in his leather jacket felt the "strength" to call me names at a gas station in Bozeman, was one of those times that didn't feel so innocent. All these thoughts and memories flooded my mind in the seconds after. I stood in silence.

"That's what I thought. Faggot. You've got nothing to say. They should brand all of you so we know. Make you wear colorful jackets or purple robes or something."

The man walked to his car and drove off. As I finished pumping my gas, I was a picture of tranquility on the outside. On the inside, though, I raged with anger, pain, hurt, disappointment...and questions.

"Why did that jerk even think..." I stopped as I walked around the back of the car to the driver's side.

"Oh. That answers that question." I shrugged out loud staring at the colorful gay-pride flag stuck to the bumper. I hadn't noticed it until now.

When I'd heard the news and wanted to see my old teacher before he passed, my car had been in the shop. So I'd borrowed my neighbor's car. He lived below me and had been happy to let me use his car for the weekend. When I circled back to the driver's side after filling the car up with gas, I noticed for the first time the colorful flag that donned the bumper.

Pulling out of the gas station and onto the I-90 on-ramp, I would like to say that the confrontation rolled off my back. Any gay man has been called names hundreds of times before reaching his late twenties. I was no different. This encounter should have been another one I chalked up to ignorance and fear, but it wasn't. It never was; not for me at least.

My mind wandered to thoughts of my teacher as I tried to push the incident out of my mind. I'd received the call yesterday. His wife said that he'd asked her to call me.

"He's not doing well," she said.

"Not doing well? What's wrong?"

The last I spoke with Mr. Smith was over six months ago. He was happy and healthy, rolling along at the ripe young age of sixty-seven.

"Heart disease," she said. Her voice sounded like she was speaking through a tin can. The sound of a woman trying to be strong, but one who found herself exhausted and broken from the last few months.

"Coronary heart disease. He had a heart attack a month ago. He was in the garage fiddling away on his car when he collapsed. Thank God I wandered out to see if he was hungry for lunch. He must have been lying there for a few minutes before I showed up.

"The paramedics said he was lucky I'd found him when I did. They rushed him to the hospital and were able to stabilize him after a few days, but the disease was too far along by that point. The doctors said they could try bypass surgery, but Al wasn't having any of it. He said he was far too old to go under the knife, especially with such a low likelihood of success in his case."

Mrs. Smith paused for what felt like a minute. I would have thought something was wrong if I couldn't hear her breathing softly on the other side of the call.

"I always hoped I'd be the first to go, but I knew better. I just didn't think it would be this soon." She paused again losing herself in thought. Mrs. Smith was always a picture of candor. No thought was too personal for her.

"Can you come see him before..." her voice trailed.

"Of course, Mrs. Smith." I was shocked. Thoughts seemed to dart through my mind, and I found myself unable to comprehend any of them. "How long..." This time it was my voice that trailed off.

"Not long," Mrs. Smith interrupted. "It could be days; it could be weeks. He won't make it to his sixty-eighth birthday two months from now, though, that's becoming clear."

"I'll be there this weekend," I assured.

"Thanks, James."

As I was hanging up the phone, I heard her say, "Oh, and James?"

"Yes, ma'am?" I said as I brought the phone back to me ear.

"Play the song for him when you're here. He'd like that."

"Mrs. Smith, I don't think..."

"He'd like that," Mrs. Smith interrupted. I understood clearly what she meant. There was no more discussion about it. She wanted me to play the song, a song I hadn't thought about for years and didn't know if I even remembered the lyrics, let alone knew if I could still play.

That was 2 P.M. yesterday. I rushed to the apartment downstairs. CJ was happy to loan me his car for the weekend. "Take it as long as you'd like," he said. Then he handed me the keys without any further questions, without even a passing wonder of where I would be taking his car.

I quickly threw a travel bag together and a small grocery bag of whatever snacks I could find laying around—two apples, a box of crackers, some fruit leather, a couple cookies leftover from a package of six, and a half eaten box of Frosted Flakes. I figured I'd grab more when I stopped for gas along the way. Then I went to look for the lyrics I had written down years ago.

I had begun to tell Mrs. Smith that I didn't remember the lyrics and didn't want to play it, which was partially true. I certainly didn't remember the lyrics to the song and I felt very uneasy at the thought of playing a silly song I wrote a decade ago, but I *had* written the lyrics down years ago when I originally wrote the stupid thing. I had three filing boxes filled with old letters, articles, class notes, and keepsakes. I had no idea in which box the slip of paper with the lyrics was, but I knew I still had it somewhere. I still don't know why I kept them so long. Maybe because I knew Mr. Smith liked it so much and that had made me proud that someone appreciated something I'd created. I don't know.

I dug through two and half boxes of notebooks and scraps of paper that I probably should have gotten rid of long ago. I finally found it—two pages of notebook paper, fringes and all, folded into a square. It sat underneath two notebooks I had kept from Mr. Smith's humanities and literature class. I'd always promised myself I'd read through them again, remembering that there were some very thought-provoking things jotted in the pages of those notebooks, but I never did. I naïvely thought maybe some day I'd need to reference them at just the right moment. Someone would need me to provide the perfect synopsis of *A Tale of Two Cities* or to succinctly explain the philosophical viewpoint of Kantian Rechtstaat, and I'd blow everyone's minds with this obscure knowledge. I never looked at those notes, though.

Between the two notebooks that sat on top of the song lyrics was a sheet of paper. At the top it read: "40 Tips for College and Life."

In the last week of our senior year, Mr. Smith knew most of us had already checked out. Since the school needed to know who was going to be walking on graduation day, the grades for the semester were already submitted. There were no more tests or papers. Some teachers pretended they could still change the grade they submitted if we didn't take the last week seriously. Our physics teacher even gave us a quiz on the second to last day. Most of us scribbled random answers on the ten-question quiz not caring about it all, but Mark Green, our valedictorian, found the entire exercise insulting.

"We're not children. Mr. Anderson's a jackass," he'd said after class, referring to our physics teacher.

On the final question, "What are Newton's Three Laws of Motion?" Mark decided he'd had enough. He wrote:

1st: An object in motion stays in motion; an object at rest stays in rest; unless an external force acts upon it, which you should understand because it doesn't look like your body has been in motion for years now.

2nd: F U = Mr. A. Whoops, that's not right. I mean... F = ma

3rd: Every action has an equal and opposite reaction. Like when a person walks, they push against the ground and the ground equally pushes back against them. Or like when our teacher is a pompous ass and gives us a quiz on the second-to-last day of our high school career, I tell him he's acting like a pompous ass.

Thanks for a great year, Mr. A!

The next day when we arrived at school for our last day of high school classes ever, the headmaster immediately pulled Mark into his office. As we walked past, we could see our Headmaster, the Dean of Boys, and Mr. Anderson all sitting around the desk before the door closed.

In the end, they didn't do much of anything to Mark. They reprimanded him "severely," Mark told us, and they made him apologize to Mr. Anderson. They also threatened to take away the valedictorian award, but everyone knew they weren't going to do that. One of our buddies somehow got his hands on the quiz and framed it. I remember seeing it in all its hilarity framed in his dorm room freshman year. I like to think about where that quiz might be now, hanging in the dorm of some new recalcitrant young know-it-all who found it in a stack of odd framed pieces at the local Goodwill, forever perpetuating the obstinate excitement that is young adolescent males.

Unlike Mr. Anderson and his physics test, Mr. Smith didn't pull any of these teacher shenanigans in the last week. Instead, we spent Monday of the last week in our first-ever class outside, basking in the spring sunlight as he lectured about the beauty of nature, the gift that it is, and how we're all called to care for it because it cares for us.

Tuesday he ordered pizza and quoted books and movies. If you guessed where the quote was from, he gave you a slice.

All the world's a stage, and all the men and women merely players...
 "As You Like It!"
 "A slice of pepperoni for the lady.'"

We don't read and write poetry because it's cute. We read and write poetry because we are members of the human race.
 "Dead Poet's Society!"
 "A piping hot slice of sausage for you, good sir."

Above all, don't lie to yourself. The man who lies to himself and listens to his own lie comes to a point that he cannot distinguish the truth within him, or around him, and so loses all respect for himself and for others. And having no respect he ceases to love.
 "The Brothers Karamazov!"
 "Would you prefer a slice of veggie or a meat lover, my dear?"

There won't be any money, but when you die, on your deathbed, you will receive total consciousness. So I got that goin' for me, which is nice.
 "Caddyshack!"
 "A piece a' pie for the scholar."

On Wednesday Mr. Smith asked us all to bring our own favorite quotes from any book or movie we read or watched while we were in high school. We all felt simultaneous excitement and pressure to come up with just the right quote—the right twinge of meaning, the right dose of humor, and the right thrust of irony. Only Mr. Smith could get a class of thirty high school kids excited about such an exercise in their last week of high school ever. That class had some of the highest participation of the year.

On Thursday of the last week of high school, Mr. Smith handed out his college advice, the same college advice I was now holding. I sat and read through each of them.

40 Tips for College and Life

1. Life's too short to not seize the opportunities with which we are presented. Always take the chance to do what you love when it comes along.
2. Question authority.
3. Question those who question authority.
4. Don't be afraid to see dinosaurs even when everyone else around you doesn't.

5. Be kind. Kindness can change things far beyond your wildest dreams. They say that absence makes the heart grow fonder, but it's kindness that makes the heart grow softer.
6. Walk barefoot through grass.
7. Be quick to show compassion and empathy.
8. Don't dress like a bum all day long.
9. Have a routine, but avoid being routine.
10. Smile.
11. We are all intelligent, thoughtful individuals. Don't let others tell you something *has to be that way*. It doesn't. The world is far too complex for it to *have to be that way*.
12. Be conscious of the present. Time is your most valuable asset.
13. It's easy to doubt. Don't be easy. Hold on to faith and hope.
14. Love a little more. You can always love more.
15. Don't jump at the first chance to go out. There will always be another party. It's college.
16. Live with purpose.
17. Not everything you do has to have *a* purpose. Folly can be quite satisfying.

18. Don't act like you know more than you actu-
    ally do. There's no shame in admitting you
    don't know the answer.

19. Remember that the things you do know are
    of value. Don't act like you know less than
    you do. Share your knowledge.

20. Don't spend each day only staring at a
    screen. Put down your phone. Close your
    laptop. Turn off your TV.

21. Share laughter. There's far too much that's
    funny out there to take yourself too serious-
    ly.

22. Share tears. There's far too much pain and
    hurt out there not to take others' struggles
    seriously.

23. Enjoy music.

24. Remember to get lost in your mind from
    time to time.

25. Breathe slowly.

26. Don't be afraid to be alone. Everyone knows:
    "Not all who wander are lost." Few realize:
    Not all who are alone are lonely.

27. Take in the beauty of nature. Look around
    you. Don't take it for granted.

28. Take in the beauty of mankind. Look around
    you and see how wonderful your neighbor
    can be.

29. Dance in the rain.

30. There will come a time in college, and in life, when you are presented with decisions that compromise your values. Know how you will respond to those times before they ever happen.

31. Have resolve.

32. Share excitement when you're excited. People who hold that against you are most likely projecting their own feelings of inadequacy.

33. Remember to read, and something more than a blog. Pick up a book from time to time.

34. There is only one you.

35. Laugh hard, kiss softly, disparage slowly, and forgive quickly.

36. Eat fully, drink deeply, and always remember to give often.

37. Decide what you believe, know who you are and live accordingly. Don't apologize to anyone for that.

38. But if you realize later on that you were wrong, admit it. Ask forgiveness.

39. Maya Angelou has a great quote: "If I'd known better, I'd have done better." We can only do the best we know how, but there's

no excuse for not striving to attain the know-how. And there's certainly no excuse for not doing better once we have it.

40. Expect Dragons.

I stared at the list thinking about how influential Mr. Smith was in my life. At a time late in my high school career when I'd felt lost and alone, he'd inspired me to believe life was full of wonder and hope. Now, just two hours before, I found out he was dying. I placed the list back into its box and slid the box back into the closet. I put the folded music lyrics into my pocket.

It was 4:25 on Thursday afternoon when I finally eased the borrowed car onto the I-84 entrance leaving Portland heading east. The sun was still shining brightly on this late spring day. I made it all the way to Missoula on the first night, pulling into a Motel 8 at a quarter past midnight.

I slept unevenly for about six hours, before I popped awake at 6 A.M. to hit the road again. There were still over sixteen hours of driving in front me before I would pull into St. Paul. I had been on the road almost three hours that morning when I'd pulled into the gas station in Bozeman. As I brought the car back onto I-90, my less than friendly encounter with the gentleman in the leather jacket and his hate-filled words left me a little shaken.

The sun shined pleasantly across the yellow fields alongside the road. In the distance out my driver's side window the mountain ranges stretched as far as I could see. When I reached cruising speed once again, a giant billboard on the side of the road caught my eye.

Time for a change? Let us help. –First Security Bank Montana

A woman in her mid-thirties smiled upon all the cars that passed under her gaze. Behind her a mountain loomed large. My thoughts were immediately jolted into a memory from my childhood, a memory I typically preferred not to recall.

"Camp Change: Let us help you change."

I could see myself sitting on the edge of my bed, an awkward thirteen year-old. A duffle bag sat at my feet. I heard my parents talking down the hall clear as day, even now as I drove along I-90.

"I don't like this at all, Jude," my mom's voice was pleading. She knew not to cross my father.

This was as defiant as her tone would ever get with him.

"What do you propose we do, Martha? What?"

The shame of a young teenage boy came rushing back to me in my car.

"Let him be a teenager," my mom's voice came back to me. "He just celebrated his thirteenth birthday. He had an excellent year in school. He was the best player on his basketball team, and his baseball coaches love him. He's just beginning to blossom as a boy."

"That's why this summer is so important, Martha!" My father's voice carried with it a hint of desperation. "Pretty soon people will begin talking. Everyone will know. No son of mine is going to be prancing around like a cheerleader or some shit. He's going to straighten up, and I mean *straighten* up."

My mom tried to counter, but my father cut her off. "No boy of mine is going to be a fairy. He just needs to get the right help. By next school year, he'll be out on the football field with the junior high team. With some dedication, he could end up playing varsity football in a few years. He just needs to be fixed."

It never seemed to matter to my father that I was actually one of the most athletic kids in my class. Somehow he had incredible blinders that allowed him only to see what he wanted to see—or maybe he just saw what he feared most. I was the point guard on my junior high basketball team and played center field on our baseball team. It didn't matter to my father. It never did.

In one basketball game my senior year in high school, we were pitted against the number one team in state in the section finals. We were heavy underdogs but managed to prevail in overtime, sending us to the state tournament. I was the point guard on that team. I dished out sixteen assists and swiped ten steals—a double-double in the most unlikely of fashions. When I got home that night, my adrenaline still rushing with excitement, I found a note on the fridge:

You couldn't even score 10 points? How could you embarrass me in front of the entire state? I'm getting drunk down the street to forget about what a disappointment you are.

The memory pained me even now. I was no longer a young boy at that point and had stopped listening to my father, so he couldn't take the wind out of my excitement from the win, but he was always able to heap shame on me with his so-called disappointment.

Again my mom's voice pulled me back into my bedroom away from that note on the fridge. I could see myself staring at my feet as I shuffled them back and forth on the carpet. My sister peered at me from her cracked door across the hall. Her eyes carried a sadness with them. "I'm sorry," she mouthed.

"Jude," my mom pleaded to my father.

"Enough!" my old man barked. Jude Hinri was the judge, jury and executioner in our house. He acted like a general at all times when it came to family matters. His father fought somewhere in Europe during World War II. My old man always made sure I knew that, but he never told me much of anything about where. My dad, however, had never served anywhere, missing forced service through the Vietnam draft by a few years. He had watched his older brother get shipped off to Vietnam, though, and never come home. Despite lacking the military training himself, my old man believed his authority was God's word in our house, and everyone knew when there would be no more questions about one of his decisions. This was one of those times.

"He doesn't need fixing," I heard my mom softly say. It was no more than a second later that I heard a loud slap and then a thud. My sister quickly shut her door, retreating to the safety she always found under her covers.

"Goddammit, Martha! Why do you make me do things like that!?!"

My dad stormed down the hall. I sat terrified on the edge of my bed. I knew the decision had been made over a week ago, but I secretly hoped my mom could sway him like she sometimes could. Now I just hoped mom was all right.

"Get your damn bag!" my dad roared. "Let's go!"

He slammed my bedroom door and then slammed the front door a few moments later. I could hear my mom crying softly down the hall and then the sound of shuffled feet coming towards my room. The door opened slowly, and my mom came in, hiding the right side of her face from me.

"I'm sorry, baby," she said sweetly as she sat down on the bed next to me. Tears rolled down her face. "I love you."

"I know, mom. I know."

I felt anger welling up inside, towards my drunk of a father, of course, but at my mother too. The feelings confused me at the time, as she sat next to me, abused by my asshole of a father. I began to learn over the years that I just wanted someone to protect me when I was a boy. I wished my mother had taken my sister and me away from that house when we were little.

"James," she said, still hiding the right side of her face.

"Yea?"

"You don't need fixing." She pulled me in close and hugged me. I felt her kiss the top of my head. What she couldn't offer in protection, my mom always gave me in acceptance. I loved her for that. "Now hurry up before he gets upset."

I wished my mom wouldn't let go. I wanted to cry, but I knew better than to bring tear-streaked cheeks into my father's truck. I grabbed my duffle bag and made my way out the front door.

"Bout time kid," my old man said as he stomped out the butt of his cigarette.

The drive to the airport couldn't have finished soon enough and, paradoxically, couldn't have lasted longer. I knew what waited for me once I climbed out of my dad's truck, but sitting in his Ford meant I had to listen to his apologies. *It's for your own good...It's because I love you...This is the best thing that will ever happen to you...You'll thank me someday...*

I didn't hear much of anything he said. I stared out the car window confused and scared. I had just finished the second semester of seventh grade with straight A's. I was the starting point guard on a basketball team filled with eighth graders. Although I was a boy entering his awkward teenage years, I felt I was starting to come into my own. I wouldn't feel that way again for a long time after that summer.

I watched the Minnesota River pass below me as we crossed the bridge toward the airport. I've come to believe that Minnesotans are some of the most tolerant and accepting people in this country, but at that moment, I hated every last one of them. In the mind of that thirteen-year-old boy, everyone in the state was my father.

As we pulled into the airport, my father reached underneath his seat and grabbed something from underneath a brown paper bag, which I could only assume contained a pint of whiskey.

"I had this made for you, son," he said as he pulled a black baseball hat out from under the bag. "See?" His words filled with pride as he showed me the cap: "Straight A's." He emphasized the word "straight."

"Thanks," I lied. To this day I still hate myself for saying thanks to that bigot for the gift. He forcefully pushed the hat onto my head. It felt like a false crown. And all I did was say, "Thanks."

"Haha!" my old man clapped his hands together. "Look at you! Looking good, son. You'll be home in no time, *straight* as an arrow and bringing in more STRAIGHT A's!" He patted me firmly on top of my head, pressing the button from the new hat hard down onto my scalp. I winced in pain. "Now get outta here. They won't hold that plane for you."

As I closed the truck door, my father leaned over to the passenger's seat and yelled out the window, "Hey son, second star on the right and STRAIGHT on 'til morning!" Then he drove off laughing happily.

"What?" I remember thinking. "That doesn't even make sense."

I flipped on the windshield wipers as my borrowed car moved across the country to my old teacher's house, momentarily shaken from my thoughts. The rain started slowly, but soon it began pouring sheets of water onto the road. I had trouble seeing more than 200 feet in front of me. Slowing the car well below the speed limit, I tried to think about anything other than that camp, but I couldn't. Soon my mind was pulled back to the day my father dropped me off at the airport.

The flight to Utah was the worst of my life. A bus was waiting for me when I landed in Salt Lake City. It was already filled with boys that looked to be as young as nine or ten and boys that were well into their late-teens, maybe even into their twenties. We drove an hour, all while the adults led us in songs that sounded vaguely Christian, until we pulled off the two-lane highway onto a dirt road. The road was lined on both sides with wooden fence posts. An arched structure greeted us as we pulled onto the road, where a banner exclaimed:

Camp Change
Gay-to-Straight
Let us help you change

I have never really told anyone about what went on that summer, and I rarely think about it. I've tried to forget it as much as I can. There was plenty of psychoanalysis— "talk therapy" they called it. I was put through a few rounds of testosterone treatments, which, they explained in the most falsely loving tone I have ever heard in my life, would allow me to become the man I was meant to be. I was thirteen.

I heard rumors that some older boys were put through electric shock therapy, or electroconvulsive therapy as it used to be called professionally, but I never saw that. I wouldn't have put it past them, though. That camp thought they were on a mission from God, and there were no means too severe to save us from perdition. We young boys were destined to be swallowed by the gates of hell, and they were doing "The Lord's Work." There was nothing they wouldn't do if it were divinely inspired.

There was constant talking at the camp. I've heard interrogation rooms with cops are brutal, but there's eventually an end to those interrogations, even if it's the next day. I was trapped. For two months I had nowhere to hide. There was no one that would listen.

"Your mother is over-bearing and your father is distant, isn't that right, son?"

"No, actually my mom is..."

"It's okay, son. It's not your fault. That's why you became gay. We're here to help. We're here to save you."

At one point they handed each of us some sort of scepter or staff. They explained it was our walking stick to change. We were required to take it with us everywhere. It went with me on every hike that summer, lay next to my bed at night, leaned against the table at meals, and sat on the ground before me as I sat cross-legged around the campfires. The irony of the Freudian, phallic reference was lost on my thirteen year-old scared mind at the time, but that scepter was always with me acting as a constant mockery of my existence.

And then there were the exercises—constant talking and always spiritual exercises. I would sit on the floor with one of my counselors behind me, the back of my head resting on his chest and his arms wrapped around me in a bear hug. Circled around me were two other counselors and four other "converts," which is what they called us. They would all stretch their hands out placing them on my head and chest. The Camp called it healing-touch-therapy. We would sing songs and chant until one of the counselors felt a "healing step" had been made.

"Great work today, son. You'll be fixed new in no time!"

I never saw any of those boys again. I have no idea if any of them were "fixed." I sure as hell wasn't. I sometimes wish I could tell those boys that I'm sorry for my participation at that camp. I know I couldn't have done anything. I was stuck there just like them, but if they were anything like me, they were just as desperate for someone to talk to. I wanted someone to understand.

When my father picked me up at the Minneapolis-St. Paul airport after two months at the camp, I was broken and alone, but much to his chagrin I was still gay. He smiled at me when I climbed into his truck. I stared at the long line of cars ahead of us at the airport. They were waiting to pick up their loved ones. I pictured grand family reunions, pleasant dinners with laughter, and joyful tears.

"Well?" my old man pushed.

I looked him dead in the eye, knowing full well what response my words would invoke, and I said, "Fuck you."

My father's hand flew up faster than I had anticipated. The backhand sent pain shooting through the right side of my face. The blood rushed, and the pain spread. He hit me so hard I could feel it in my toes.

"All right!" My old man clapped his hands, surprising me. "Looks like we can still make a man outta you, boy. Standing up for yourself. It's about time!"

The drive home was silent. When we pulled into the driveway, my mom stood on the front steps waiting anxiously. Her face had healed from the bruises that were forming when I left. It looked as if the bruises had simply thrown themselves from her face onto mine. My right eye had begun to swell. I could see my mom's eyes begin to well up as she turned back into the house.

I heard that camp closed a number of years ago. I had seen a news story online in the *New York Times*. A sixteen-year-old whose parents had forced him to attend the camp was interviewed for the story. A huge investigation commenced, and the Utah Department of Children's Services concluded that there was no sign of child abuse. Someone at the DEA, though, got wind of things. He must have been upset by the notion of the camp because he started sniffing around and discovered that unlicensed staff had been administering prescription drugs. After God knows how long this camp went on and all the boys they ruined, it wasn't abuse that led to their demise but prescription drugs. It was like busting Al Capone for tax evasion.

The camp was shut down not long after that. Soon national papers ran stories about other camps and straight retreat centers as they were exposed one by one. One young journalist posed as a young gay man who wanted to become straight. He infiltrated an extended weekend camp in Tennessee and wrote a 3,000-word exposé on what he experienced there. People were furious and eventually...

Huuunnnhhh! Huuunnnhhh!

A semi truck blared its horn and shook me from my daze. I was riding the lane to my right pretty hard. I quickly jerked the car left and leaned down to wave up to him apologetically. He didn't seem to care, shaking his fist at me angrily as if he was in the 1920s driving a Model T. It didn't bother me. His angry horn jerked me from a nightmare I'd been trying to forget for most of my life now. I accelerated past the semi.

The rain had now ceased, and the sun was shining brightly. A hunger I had been ignoring for a while suddenly crept over me. My stomach growled angrily. "Join the club," I said to my stomach, nodding at the semi fading from view in my mirror.

Ten miles down the road I eased my car off the highway into the small town of Miles City. I had already been on the road almost seven hours. I stretched my legs and looked down Main Street. *Small town America indeed*, I thought to myself. *This is quaint.* Two water towers gently stood watch over the town. The sun glistened off the metal as trees surrounded the base of one of the towers as if they were the subjects below. A few strained to grow taller and enter the heights of the tower, which bore the town's name in white letters across the side.

I strolled into a local diner, stretching my muscles and joints with each step. My back was aching from sitting so long. This drive seemed easy ten years ago. Now, it was much harder on my body.

Age waits for no one, they say. I'm still quite young, but I'm beginning to realize what they mean. In the annals of time, age remains undefeated, no losses to date.

I quickly scarfed down a grilled cheese and fries. I hadn't realized how hungry I actually was until I stepped out of the car. My mind tried to drift back to the camp from years ago, but I wasn't going to let that happen again. I'm not interested in more memories from that summer. When the waitress asked if I had room for dessert, I ignored my better judgment and ordered a chocolate milk shake for the road.

After filling my tank again, I grabbed a water and a few snacks from the gas station. I tried to make a call, but my cell service was at one bar. I saw a pay phone on the side of the gas station and grabbed a few quarters from the change tray in my car. *I always wondered who still used these things*, I thought as I dialed.

"Hi, Mrs. Smith." I greeted her with the concerned tone of someone unsure what emotion I should be projecting.

"James!" Mrs. Smith responded. Her voice contained far more excitement than I expected for someone whose husband of forty-two years was dying in the next room. "Don't tell me you have bad news!" she chided as her voice remained chipper.

"No, no, Mrs. Smith. Well, not additional bad news beyond the news of Mr. Smith's..."

"Good! How's the drive?"

"It's fine. I'm in a little place called Miles Town or Miles City or something. I'm at the eastern end of Montana."

"Good. Good to hear it, James. So how much longer do you have on the open road?" She said those last words as if I were a lost traveler searching for a home to rest his head.

"I'll make it to Bismark tonight for sure," I said as I looked at the clock on my phone, which let me know it was almost 4:00 P.M. "I think I might even try to make it to Fargo, but that's probably pushing it. I should get to your place sometime tomorrow afternoon, Mrs. Smith."

"That's great. Al is so happy you're coming. His face lit up when I told him yesterday that you were making the drive." She paused, listening to see if her husband had called her from the next room. After feeling confident that she only imagined it, she continued, "You're going to play your song, right James? Al tuned his guitar for the first time in weeks last night. I didn't say anything to him, but I think he's hoping you'll play it for him."

"I found the old lyrics in a box I had in the closet, Mrs. Smith, but I don't know why you want me to play that stupid song anyway. It's so…"

"Because he likes it, James," she interrupted. "He likes it. Isn't that enough?"

"I guess it should be," I thought, but my own doubts and insecurities always left me uncomfortable playing music for others. I remembered a time in high school when Mr. Smith stared in wonder at another teacher. "Look at her," he said in excitement. I looked to see another teacher mesmerized by a coffee mug.

"Yea….? So, what's she looking at?"

"The coffee mug," he answered without breaking his gaze at his co-worker across the room.

"I….see that," I replied slightly annoyed. "Why?" I was baffled why his gaze was fixed on his homely, sixty-year-old colleague.

"I don't know," was his matter-of-fact response, "but she's so captivated by it. It's fascinating."

"You all right, Mr. Smith?"

He looked away from her and directed his gaze toward me. He smiled wistfully—a look I had learned meant he was about to impart some wisdom on me.

"You see how excited she is don't you?"

I nodded.

"Well, that's interesting. Here she is, looking at something as simple and unimportant as a coffee mug, yet she's captivated by it. That excites me. I have no idea why she's captivated, but I still know that she is, just from the expression on her face."

He leaned back in his chair. "You see, James, she finds that coffee mug interesting for some reason. I have no idea why, but the mere fact that she finds it so fascinating is interesting in and of itself. Other people's excitement should bring us excitement, son. Always remember that.

"There's nothing wrong with letting someone else's sense of wonder spill over into you. This applies ten-fold when it's someone you care about dearly. Allow their passions to be your passions. Experience life with those you love, and let their interests excite you, even if they're not your primary interest, even if it's just a coffee mug. It allows for a much more enriching life, James."

He got up and walked off with a smile.

I was reminded of this encounter with Mr. Smith as his lovely wife was insisting I play the song for him tomorrow. I knew what Mr. Smith would say. I knew he'd urge that his enjoyment of the song should be enough for me to enjoy it.

An electronic voice in the handset notified me that my time was running out.

"Are you on a pay phone, James?" Mrs. Smith chuckled.

"Yea, sounds like my time's almost up, and I'm out of quarters. I'll see..."

The dial tone boorishly cut our conversation short. I hung up the receiver with mild disgust and strolled back to my car. I drove back down Main Street and whimsically thought about a different life here—a small town boy growing up in small town America. I would have been the town hero leading us to state championships in basketball and baseball. Maybe I would have even tried my hand at soccer. I would drive down Main Street just like this, and everyone would wave to me. "There goes James Hinri!" they would announce. I would nod and smile and impart my wisdom onto the younger generations.

It was a nice daydream, but I doubted a small town like this would accept a boy like me. Still, I enjoyed the dream.

I heard church bells announcing the four P.M. hour as I rolled down my windows. It was a little over six hours to Fargo. With another time zone change, it would be after 11:00 P.M. when I got there, even if I hurried. I decided not to push it and to stop in Bismarck for the night. *So long Miles City,*

I thought as I passed the church, turned off Main Street, and hopped back onto the interstate.

It had been years since I'd stepped foot in a church. I consider myself spiritual, but I had a hard time participating in a religion that poured shame and rebuke upon me, especially in my impressionable teenage years. After a while, its insistence that it didn't want to be affiliated with someone like me convinced me that maybe it was right; maybe we shouldn't be affiliated with each other anymore. I couldn't help but think of the old Groucho Marx line, though. How's it go? I don't care to belong to any club that will accept people like me as a member? I think that's it. Maybe a religion like that is exactly what old Groucho was looking for. I couldn't do it. Be kind and accepting to all God's creatures, except to the homos; at least that's what I was hearing all those years.

One of the last times I went to church, long before I officially "came out"—although I suspect most people knew well before then, hell, my parents sent me to that camp at thirteen—I remember feeling a tremendous sense of peace. My good friend Matt and I owned our own yard maintenance company the summer after we graduated from high school. "Wuri Free Yards." We thought the misspelling of the word "worry" would capture

people's eyes. We certainly weren't marketing geniuses, that's for sure.

We had just finished up a long day of mowing,
trimming, edging, and weeding one yard after another. As we neared 5 P.M. storm clouds rolled in,
and it began to rain as we finished our final yard of
the day. We loaded our equipment up in the rain
and decided to attend the evening service. We always kept extra shirts in the trunk, but our shoes
had gotten muddy, so we decided to enter the
church sans shoes. We thought it was very Jesus-
esque.

I remember being filled with a peaceful perma-
nence as I sat there. I had just finished four years
of high school, an accomplishment in and of itself
when it came to my family lineage. I had my own
yard maintenance company that I'd started that
summer. I was staring at the prospect of college in
a few short months. I felt very gratified by where I
was at that point in my life, but at that moment I
was neither looking back nor staring ahead. I was
just pleased to be exactly where I was. I was peaceful.

Little did I know that I was causing inner turmoil for the woman sitting in the pew in front of
me. When the service ended, she turned around

and glared with utter disdain. "You two disgust me," she glowered.

I was terrified. I thought, "She knows! The jig is up. She's terribly mistaken about my friend Matt, here, but she found me out." I often thought my gay-ness, as I used to think about it, was noticeable to everyone, as if there were a bumper sticker on my back like the one on the back of the car. I was relieved to realize she hadn't found me out.

"You hippies, with your dirty pants and nasty bare feet. This is a place of worship!" As she admonished us, she poked a finger into my chest and spit flew from her lips at my face. "Have some respect."

She then knelt down for another session of abject prayer.

That wasn't the last time I had walked into a church, but it certainly didn't help the perception that I wasn't welcome.

The fields continued to roll by outside my window. Mile after mile, the same flat scene presented itself to me. Very few cars drove along I-94 beside me. Prairie field after prairie field stretched as far as I could see, a pleonastic discourse in the form of the American countryside. Western Montana is a beautiful sight with its looming mountains and the quintessential depiction of the great wide open.

Eastern Montana, however, has the graceful presence of a cornfield without the corn. I seemed alone on the road.

I found myself becoming weary with the open road and the vapid scenery out my windows. I rubbed my eyes, bleary from the constant beating of the sun off the pavement as it dropped down in the sky in my rearview mirror. Dusk quickly turned to night, and darkness covered the surrounding scenery, which wasn't a disappointment. I saw a sign letting me know Bismarck was fifty-two miles away and decided I would make a quick stop to shake off the doldrums brought on by a full day of driving.

I filled the car up with gas for the drive tomorrow and grabbed a few snacks, including the obvious road-trip choice of an extra long Slim Jim and Coke for a jolt of caffeine to sustain me through the final stretch of road for the day. I stopped at a row of four turnstiles filled with trinkets and souvenirs. Throwing on a pair of knockoff Ray Bans, I grabbed a camouflage hat that read "Get Bent" across the front. Smiling at the ridiculousness of the cap, I knew I would never wear it for even a moment, and it quickly found its way back onto the rack.

"No sir!" came a booming voice from behind me. "This is the one you want."

A man who stood at least 6'3" with a face that hadn't been beardless for what was probably years came from behind the counter. He grabbed another camouflaged hat, this one a trucker hat with mesh in the back.

"No homo!" he exclaimed as he placed the hat atop my head.

I looked into the tiny mirror on the rack. "No Homo," the hat read backwards in the mirror. He pushed it down hard and pulled the bill to straighten it out, jerking my head and neck forward.

"There ya go, son. Look at yourself there. That's the one you want."

I peered back into the tiny three-inch mirror and as I did, I felt betrayed. The burly man grabbed the Slim Jim from my hand and slapped me on the top of the head with it in what surely he must have thought was a friendly manner. It was harder than I would have liked, though, and I winced from the sharp pain in my scalp. He marched back behind the counter whistling.

"All of these things?" he said as he scanned the jerky and motioned for me to put everything else on the counter.

"Ahh, yea," I hesitated, "except the terrible hat. I think I'll go without that."

"Suit yourself, son. That's a strong hat, though. Keeping the sunglasses?"

"Yes sir," I said as I dropped the other snacks and soda on the counter. I walked back to my car and quickly got back on the road. On a different day, one where I hadn't been driving for twelve hours, I might have said something more to the man, but on this day I found myself too tired to care. What would be the point?

I quickly chugged the coke. I could see the flatness of the land around me, but the dark night prevented me from seeing how far it reached. I had seen North Dakota before. There was no need for me to see it again.

Describing the North Dakota scene along I-94 with anything more than saying it made eastern Montana look divine would be a disservice to Montana. Farmland stretched in both directions from the highway. The interstate dipped and rose in front of me, but never turned in the slightest. If ever someone was foolish enough to think cruise control meant the car would drive itself, this appeared to be the road on which they might actually succeed. It was a straight shot to the eastern edge of North Dakota.

I pushed through the final hour and pulled into Bismarck exhausted. I reeked from sitting in a car all day. I spent no time trying to find the right motel and pulled into the first one I saw on the side of the road. I got the key to my room and quickly crashed in my bed.

I had meant to call Mrs. Smith one more time when I reached my hotel, but as the sun peeked through my motel curtains, I realized I had forgotten. It was probably better anyway, since it was so late when I arrived last night. I decided I would get on the road, and I would call along the way if I found a phone. I was eager to get going, knowing today I would see my favorite teacher again, probably for the last time.

I quickly showered and grabbed some drab coffee in a styrofoam cup by the front office. The sun had already been up for a few hours when I hit the road today. I had decided to nab a little extra sleep and didn't begin driving until after 8 A.M. I made good time to Fargo, crossing the Minnesota border around 10:30. I waved goodbye to the North Dakota countryside without the slightest hint of sadness to see it go.

As I-94 veered to the southeast, I reminisced about Mr. Smith and the care he always had for me as a teacher. I realized that I had been so determined to make my way from Portland to St. Paul that I hadn't given much thought to what we would talk about. Except for that song—why did he even like that song?—I hadn't thought about what I would do when I saw him. What would he look like? Was Mr. Smith wasting away? Was he losing his mental faculties? I hadn't the faintest idea.

The sun was once again shining brightly by the 11 A.M. hour. My mind darted from one thought to the next without finding anything worthwhile on which to fixate. Flipping through radio stations, my fingers quickly halted the seek function on my radio dial when it hit a local college station. I became lost in the sound streaming through my speakers. There was raw emotion in their instruments and an authentic enjoyment in their voices. A moment ago I was nervously pondering what would probably be my last meeting with the man who had always been my ebullient teacher, wondering whether he would no longer have that effervescent aura he'd always had; and now I found myself lost in some classic road trip mise en scène. Unplanned and organic, I sat awash in both the music and the wind rushing through my windows.

I glimpsed the sign speeding past me to my right: "St. Paul 49 Miles." I eased the car onto the exit ramp for one last fill-up and to call Mrs. Smith.

"Hi, James! Is everything all right? Should we be expecting you soon?"

"Hi, Mrs. Smith. Everything is great. I think I'm about forty-five minutes away. I stopped to get gas, and I figured I would grab a late lunch."

"Nonsense! I'll prepare lunch. We haven't eaten yet ourselves, so we'll just wait another hour. You should make it here a little after two. It'll be perfect timing."

"I appreciate that, Mrs. Smith, but there's no need to go to the trouble."

I found myself hoping she would insist upon lunch at their place. I was tired of the fast food and the snacks that had sustained me for two days on the road since Thursday afternoon. My fingers ran across the coiled metal cord of the payphone that had probably been unwashed since before I had moved away from Minnesota nearly a decade ago. I looked at my fingers, which were all of a sudden feeling grimy and diseased, and wiped them on jeans.

"It's no trouble at all, James. We can enjoy the sunny weather on the porch."

I hesitated for a moment, trying to find the best way to ask my next question.

"Ummm...Mrs. Smith?"

"Yes?"

"Should I be prepared for anything? I mean, well, how does Mr. Smith look? How is..."

"You'll be pleasantly surprised, James. He's having a great day. He looks as spry as the last time you saw him, for the most part. He tires easy, but Al is as magnetic as he's always been."

She paused for a moment and then chirped, "Well, no sense wasting time chit-chatting on the phone when I can see you in the flesh all too soon. Hurry up, James!"

With that, she hung up. I was back on the road with mile markers and billboards whizzing past. My excitement to see Mr. Smith again, coupled with the anxiety that comes from knowing you're seeing someone you love for what might be the last time, grew with each passing mile.

As the wind kissed my face, my mind drifted to another time. I was standing at the front door with my mom, a large duffle bag and a backpack in hand. My sister hugged me tightly as she tried to hold back the tears. She smiled sheepishly. We had spent a lot of time together over the summer. The night before we'd talked late into the night. Her experience growing up was drastically different than mine. As a straight girl, my father chose to mostly leave her alone. My mom wouldn't have allowed for any kind of abuse to her anyway. Me, on the other hand, I was fair game. There was an unspoken and antiquated view that my rearing, as a son, belonged primarily to my father; and the abuse, both psychological and physical, was frequent.

My sister apologized that she'd had a much better childhood than I'd had. I told her she deserved a childhood every bit as wonderful and better. It was a great night together, one I won't ever forget.

She hugged me at the front door. I was heading off to college and saying goodbye to the house that raised me. I was saying goodbye to the mother and sister that I loved dearly. I was saying goodbye to the father who'd always wished I was something different, who'd always wished I was some*one* different.

"There he goes! Behold the man! My gay son off to fight the world!" He wandered into the kitchen to grab another beer from the fridge. On his way back to his leather throne in front of the TV, he rubbed my head.

"I'm just kidding ya, James. I'm just pulling your chain!" His tone insisted that he believed this to be true. Despite years of evidence to the contrary, my father seemed to think that he was actually kidding when he said things like that. He seemed to think that his ignorance and, if I was being honest, hatred didn't betray him even now.

"Why should I care if you're gay?" he continued as if someone had pressed him to elaborate on his feelings, which, of course, no one did. We had all grown tired of it years ago.

"I couldn't care less, James." He took a sip of his newly-opened beer. "Who am I to judge if my son is gay? Let him without sin cast the first stone, right? There's nothing wrong with it as long as you don't act on it, James. You know that's always what I've thought. Everything I've done in my life has been in support of you, son. We all have our vices and impulses; yours are no different, no matter how you try to twist it to feel better about yourself."

He paused a long while, continuing to sip his beer regularly. He hadn't looked away from the TV throughout his entire speech. I'm not sure I'd even call it that. Calling it a speech is probably an insult to other speeches throughout history. There are terrific orators rolling over in their graves at the thought of it even being considered a speech.

My old man finally glanced away from the television and looked up at me longingly. I could see he wished to connect with me, but he just couldn't bring himself to take that step. He went as far as he could go in his mind, and I knew that.

"Don't say I never taught you anything," he concluded.

"Thanks, Dad. You certainly are unrivaled in your support," I smiled derisively. I gave my mom a kiss as I grabbed by bags and stepped outside.

That was the last time I saw my father. Two months before Christmas that year my mom found him lifeless on the kitchen floor. I attended the unceremonious funeral, more to support my mom than to say my goodbyes to the man with whom I shared DNA. I had said goodbye to him years ago, bit by bit, slowly and gradually. I didn't need a funeral and burial to say my final goodbyes.

Before I left town that day for college, making the reverse of the same drive I was making now, I stopped by Mr. Smith's house. I wanted to thank him once again for inspiring me in class each day. He knew how much I appreciated his efforts as a teacher. There was always an enkindling incorruptibility in his daily lessons. During a time in my life when I was losing hope for the good and the beautiful in the world, when I was ready to conclusively decide that it was all a crock, Mr. Smith found a small spark of wonder that still remained somewhere deep inside me. He didn't point it out to me in an effort to convince me that I should remain hopeful. He didn't even galvanize me to save that spark of hope before it went out and I became completely jaded to the world.

Instead, he simply fanned it, very gently at first. Over time, that spark grew into a fire once again. I wasn't the only student whom Mr. Smith saved, so to speak, over the years either. Year after year, Mr. Smith's classes received the highest marks in student reviews. He had a knack for inspiring his students to see life not as it is, but as they want it to be. Outsiders saw it as naiveté, but Mr. Smith didn't care. As a child stares at a butterfly or as an infant watches running water for the first time, that's how Mr. Smith wanted all his students to look at the world. He never wanted us to lose that sense of wonder. He managed to enkindle that within my imagination.

On the day I was leaving town to head out west, the last day I ever saw my father, Mr. Smith asked how the goodbye with my parents went. He knew all about the relationship I had with my father. He was unsurprised by the interaction. When I told him about my old man's "honorable" restraint from casting the first stone, he furrowed his brow and took on a mocking tone, conjuring up his best southern preacher impersonation.

"Crucify them! Crucify them! Love the sinner, but hate the sin, brotha. As long as they have sin within them, we must do everything to cast it out of them. This is a matter of life and death, my people! The way is hard and narrow. We hate them to save their souls. And for the children! Oh, the children! Won't anybody think about the children?!" He was laying it on thick now, his tone even more mocking than when he had started.

Taking a breath, Mr. Smith stared off down his tree-lined street. "What a crock," he concluded solemnly.

Then he looked me dead in the eyes, his demeanor changing in an instant. "James, no one can ever take away your fervor. That steadfast desire to affect change? That kind heart? That's yours and yours alone. Protect it at all cost and share it with unabashed hope. Don't let anyone—Anyone!—convince you otherwise."

I hugged Mr. Smith and hopped into my car to head west.

Now, as my car reached the Twin Cities after a long drive back east, I reflected on how many times I had doubted Mr. Smith's words over the years. Time and again I'd found myself skeptical that hope was actually as powerful as he said. I doubted whether how I lived my life really had any effect on the world around me at all.

As I turned down Mr. Smith's street, I realized that somewhere in the last few years I had not only doubted the advice he'd given me as a young man, but that I had stopped caring about it altogether. I had become complacent to whether my actions, good or bad, even mattered at all.

I eased the borrowed car into the driveway. Mrs. Smith was already in the front doorway smiling. She was carrying a platter of sandwiches, which she placed on the small table on the front porch. Wiping her hands on the apron around her waist, she strolled down the front walk. This lovely old woman exuded a copacetic feeling of welcome. I embraced her halfway up the walk.

"It's so great to have you, James."

Her hands rested on my biceps. I watched her eyes well up and found mine following suit.

"Of course," I replied, with no further thoughts formulating in my mind. After over two full days in the car, with only the road and my thoughts to keep me company, I found myself unable to conjure up a more coherent response.

"C'mon," she said as she clasped her arm within mine and turned back up the front walk. "Come sit on the porch. Al is so excited."

I sat alone on the porch looking out to the street. The sun shone brightly. I leaned forward with my face pointed upward to let it wash over me. The warmth felt nice for a moment before I leaned back into the cool shade of the porch. I could hear faint sounds of struggle behind me within the house. Moments later, Mrs. Smith emerged with a pitcher of lemonade and a pitcher of iced tea. She placed both onto the table next to three glasses and the sandwiches.

"I'll bring out some ice in a moment, Hun," she said as she whisked herself back into the house.

After another few minutes alone, I heard the two of them struggling down the hall. I pictured a frail old man unable to move on his own accord, arm draped around the woman he had loved for so many years, leaning on her fragile frame for support. It was at this moment, as I sat wondering why the hell I wasn't the one inside helping Mr. Smith make his way to the front porch, when I heard his booming voice.

"James, my boy! How are ya?!"

The man I saw emerge from the doorway was neither feeble nor weak. Sure, he looked thinner than ever, but the man I had just imagined was nowhere in sight.

"Mr. Smith," I stammered, "You...you look great."

"Ahh, James, c'mere and give me a hug."

Mr. Smith wrapped his strong arms around my neck and pulled me close. He felt thin. The disease had clearly been affecting his diet, but he still had impressive strength in his grip.

"You think I look great because you see with your heart and not your eyes, James," the old man laughed. "You always did see what's on the inside, but you needn't lie. I look like crap. I know full well that I look skinnier than a clothesline. If I'm not tethered to the porch, a strong breeze might blow me away like a sheet in the wind. Haha!"

He motioned to the chairs at the end of the porch. "Sit! Sit, James! Maria made us some delicious sammies. In my younger days I might have been excited for some day drinking—you and I getting *three* sheets to the wind." His voice trailed off wistfully.

The three of us made our way to the end of the porch. Mr. Smith settled in on his cushioned glider in the corner. With the table between us, I sat across from him. Mrs. Smith sat on a small folding chair with her back to the street. I tried to give her the other glider, but she insisted.

"You know where that term comes from, don't you, James? Three sheets to the wind?" Mr. Smith inquired knowing full well that I hadn't the slightest idea. This man who had so greatly influenced my life had a mind full of knowledge and seemingly useless facts. He was a walking, human encyclopedia.

"No sir, but I'm sure you're going to enlighten me."

"Mmm," Mr. Smith nodded. "Maria, could you be a doll and make me an Arnold Palmer?"

"Of course, dear," his doting wife replied. She quickly mixed Mr. Smith a drink of lemonade and iced tea, being sure to put more iced tea in the mix than lemonade because, as Mr. Smith was apt to say to anyone who questioned, a true Arnold Palmer, the way that old Arnie himself created it, is meant to be more iced tea than lemonade.

Arnold Palmer loved the drink after hot days on the golf course, I've heard my teacher wax on in the past. He typically liked to drink iced tea, but on really hot days, adding some lemonade into iced tea was his drink of choice. Most people think it's half-and-half, but it ain't, not as The King himself liked it at least. The greatest golfer alive, with seven majors to his name, and he still has the time to create one of the greatest drinks ever invented.

Hot dog! He would always clap his hands together when he said "hot dog."

My old teacher was never one for hyperbole, but when it came to a few topics like sustainable energy, *The Great Gatsby*, and Arnold Palmer, hyperbole became second nature. He spoke about Arnold Palmer as if the two had been friends for years, which, of course, they hadn't. I made the mistake once of noting to Mr. Smith that by any concrete measure of the sport of golf, both Jack Nicklaus and Tiger Woods were stronger golfers historically. I found myself lost in a thirty-minute diatribe of Palmer's greatest accomplishments and the fact— and don't try to argue that it was clearly opinion and not fact—that Nicklaus and Woods would have never had careers if Palmer hadn't propelled the game of golf into heights previously unseen in the newfound television era.

On this day, I knew far better than to open the door for Arnold Palmer worshipping. I wanted to sit on this porch for hours with the old man, but I didn't want to spend it debating the less than finer points of golf.

After filling his glass, Mrs. Smith glanced at me as if to say, should I make you a drink too, to which I nodded politely. The air was soft and clear. We all leaned back in our chairs. There were turkey, ham, and bologna sandwiches on a platter cut into triangles. I grabbed myself a bologna for old time's sake.

"The term, my boy, is a nautical one. Three sheets to the wind refers to the ropes that control the trim of a sail. If one of the ropes, or sheets, are loose, the sail flaps much more uncontrolled, and the ship rocks with it. Some people will tell you that the term refers to the sheets on a clotheslines or the canvas panes on a windmill or any other number of bogus explanations, but they're wrong."

He took a long drink. "The phrase used to be one of degrees. The more sheets that were loose, or 'to the wind', up to four sheets, the more violently the boat would rock uncontrolled like a drunken sailor. Eventually the phrase became known simply as 'three sheets to the wind.' Interesting stuff, isn't it, James?"

"It always is, sir," I responded with a smile.

"If anyone questions the authenticity of that, tell them they don't have to believe you, but they sure as hell have to believe Admiral William Henry Smyth, who wrote about it posthumously in his 1867 alphabetical digest of nautical terms. He was quite a man, Smyth was. And what a way to go. He takes his grandson out to look at Jupiter through his telescope, a remarkable sight even today, let alone in the 1860's, and then dies of a heart attack a few hours later. That's how I'd like to go, my friend—doing the things that I've always done. Just living my life."

I grabbed two more sandwiches as I listened to Mr. Smith. I was immediately reminded of his old classes. He would effortlessly flow from story to story, weaving books and history and religion and music all seamlessly together in a fine tapestry of a lecture. I felt as if I were in the middle of one of his classes now.

"His obituary was perfect, too!" he continued.

He was always genial and courteous, ever keeping things in happy order, and by his ready wit and flow of humor compelling the maintenance of good fellowship. He used to fill his pockets with new half-pennies to distribute to any children he met in his daily walks. Whatever he did, he did it with his might.

"That's spectacular! Short and sweet. A man of humor and filled with kindness. I could only be so lucky!"

"Dear," interrupted Mrs. Smith with a smile, "don't get yourself too worked up. Try one of the sandwiches."

Mr. Smith took a small bite of a ham sandwich that had been sitting on the napkin on his lap since we sat down. Crumbs fell from his lips onto his sweater. Mrs. Smith quickly rose to her feet and brushed the crumbs into her own napkin. The two smiled at each other longingly.

"How do you know a random nineteenth century obituary of an unknown admiral?" I asked.

"James, my boy, computers are a wonderful tool, but they're making people dumber because they're no longer being used as just a tool. Information at your fingertips? We'll see about that. This is the real power behind a computer," he said as he tapped his forefinger on the side of his head. "An active and oft exercised brain has been proven to fight any number of maladies as we age—memory loss, dementia, Alzheimer's, depression... People don't think anymore!

"Besides, there's value in memorization beyond just a healthy brain. As the great Spanish writer George Santayana said, 'Those who cannot remember the past are condemned to repeat it.' That, my friend, is as true as truth can be. Our history informs our future.

"Don't waste your brain, James! It can save you from the mistakes of our past and keep you from forgetting things in the present. A well-exercised brain prevents all sorts of illnesses!" He paused momentarily before slowing his speech. "Unfortunately, it doesn't help the heart at this point, does it."

"Dear..." a concerned Mrs. Smith leaned in.

Mr. Smith stared off into nothing. His brow was furrowed, considering something he clearly wasn't inclined to share with his wife or myself. The porch held the long silence until I felt the need to break the hush.

"Mrs. Smith, these sandwiches are delicious. What's the spread on here? I thought it was mayo, but it clearly isn't."

"Oh, James. You're too kind."

"It's got a slight spiciness to it. I never thought a simple sandwich could be so delicious. What is that?"

"I'll never tell," she smiled coyly. "People overdo sandwiches. There's an art to simplicity."

"It's certainly an art when you do it." I leaned in to help myself to another ham and a turkey. The Arnold Palmer tasted as good as the sandwiches, a perfect accompaniment. Were my heightened senses from being with my old teacher making everything taste better? Was I more conscious of simple tastes because I didn't want to miss a moment?

A breeze began to pick up and blew the branches in the trees lining the front street. A man walking his dog along the boulevard waved as he passed.

"Hey Al, beautiful day, isn't it?"

"Aren't they all?" Mr. Smith replied, waving as the man passed. "Don't be a stranger!"

The man smiled and went on his way. Mrs. Smith began to clean up the plates. She grabbed the last bite of the one sandwich Mr. Smith feigned to eat and frowned at him as she brushed crumbs off his sweater. As she carried dishes back into the house, Mr. Smith reached his hand across the table and grabbed mine.

"You're a good man, James Hinri. I'm so glad you made the trip." He winked at me as he said it. Then he hollered to his wife inside the house, "Maria, can you..."

"One step ahead of you, Dear," she interrupted. She returned a minute later with arms free of lunch plates and her hands carrying a guitar. My heart sank with nervous dread. I knew this moment was coming, but I somehow hoped we would all forget.

"I love you, Dear," Mr. Smith clapped. "James, my boy, I've tuned my old friend to perfection for you."

"Oh, I don't know, Mr. Smith." I stammered, still hoping I could avoid playing. "Let's not ruin a beautiful afternoon."

"Nonsense! This will only add to my excitement about today. What's it called again? Message...?" He paused, trying to come up with the words.

"Message for No One," I replied with deflated breath. "I haven't played it in forever, Mr. Smith. It's something I wrote when I was young and naïve." I reluctantly grabbed the guitar from Mrs. Smith, who had been holding it out to me since she walked back out to the porch and was clearly growing tired of extending her arms to me. "I don't know why you like it anyway."

"I could explain it to you, James, but quite frankly, I don't care if you know why I like the song. I like it. That should be enough to share a piece of yourself with someone for whom you care. Now, don't make me wait any longer. I've been dying to hear you play this song for me, unfortunately, quite literally."

He meant that last line as a playful dose of humor, but it fell flat with melancholic gloom. My instincts still were to argue, but I knew better at this point. I strummed a few chords while staring at my toes. I felt Mrs. Smith's smile beaming in my direction, but I refused to meet her eyes. A feeling of unnecessary fear permeated my brain.

"Go ahead, James," Mrs. Smith cooed as gently as the breeze that rustled the leaves.

I cleared my throat, still in unnecessary panic. I began plucking a variation of a C and then sang the song that Mr. Smith, to my surprise, had always loved.

Message for No One

There's a call on the telephone, but I don't know who it's from
The voice on the other side leaves a message for no one
A promise of another life, one that's better than mine
I wish I could take so I won't fall all the time
Lost and forsaken unable to change
Standing all alone with no one left to blame
But somehow there's got to be more there for me
I can't believe this is all my life can be
In such a big world, I feel so small
A message for no one, I missed my call

The clock stops its tick tocks a man frozen in time
A life dead already with no answers to why
But somehow there's someone there no one can see
A man now blind who once was free

Pieces Like Pottery

Two wars fought past and bravery hast what could take
that life away?
One loss too many and regrets from yesterday
He once had things to say but no one ever heard
A widening gyre of loss when will we ever learn
If someone would listen and break down this wall
A message for no one, I missed my call

But something's going down
And no one's left around
Something's got to give before all the streams run dry
If all there is is life and death, then I'm living a lie
It's all a lie

Tobacco shops filled with cops
Hair salons filled with ex-cons
Hollywood does what it should
And the White House helps to work things out
You and me, soon we'll see
There's more to this life than we perceive
And all the games we seem to play
Well in the end they just fade away

A world turned upside down worth living my life for
One by one they all sign up and you've got my support
The calming breeze, the greener trees, the mountains
looming high

With faces fair and the warm air, then we'll have arrived
If someone would listen, I won't feel so small
A message for no one, I can't miss my call
Can't miss my call
Can't miss my call
I can't miss my call

The last note reverberated underneath the porch roof and off the front of the house. No one said a thing. A dog barked down the street. I immediately regretted playing the song again. The silence on the porch, while in reality only a few seconds, felt like minutes.

"Bravo!" Mr. Smith clapped. "That was wonderful! Thank you, James"

He leaned back smiling whimsically. "That was absolutely wonderful. You brought a smile to a dying old man's face, James. Not many people in the world can likely say that today."

He sat for a while with his eyes closed in silence while I continued to stare down at my feet. Then he looked over to me, "It's time for my old bones to take a nap now. That performance will imbue my daytime dreams."

"He tires easily these days," Mrs. Smith smiled apologetically as she helped Mr. Smith to his feet. As they passed by me toward the front door, Mrs.

Smith paused momentarily in front of me and touched my knee. "That was delightful, James. Just delightful."

The two lovebirds of forty-two years shuffled into the house as Mr. Smith faintly whistled the chorus of my song. After a few minutes of sitting on the porch alone, Mrs. Smith came back out to show me my room.

"I'll be in the sun porch if you need anything, James." Then she left me.

I set my bags on the dresser next to the bed and decided I would lie down as well. The twenty-six hour drive over two and a half days had exhausted me. I climbed under a crocheted quilt and found myself drifting off to sleep rather quickly.

When I woke up, the daylight was just beginning to fade. I looked at my phone and saw I had been asleep nearly three hours. A little stunned and more so embarrassed that I had slept through much of the late afternoon, I made my way to the kitchen rubbing my bleary eyes. I found Mrs. Smith at the counter preparing spaghetti for dinner.

"Al just laid back down for another nap, James. He promised he would be up for dinner, but I don't think we should plan on it." Her voice was sad and weary.

I smiled kindly. "Can I help with dinner?" She shook her head, but I persisted. "Let me help at least with something."

Her tone perked up slightly with her response. "No, James, not because I don't want to have a guest in my house doing any work, but because I don't want my dinner ruined." Only Mrs. Smith could insult someone with a smile and leave that person feeling like he wasn't, in fact, insulted.

I decided to take a walk around the neighborhood in the fading light. The streets crisscrossed in a tangled maze. I gazed into front windows as families throughout the neighborhood enjoyed dinner together. I wandered aimlessly down one street to the next. The shady lanes cast a fable-like character to the neighborhoods. I peered at each family longingly. One by one they gathered in the place they called home.

I had been searching for my own place to call home. I had been searching for my own sense of belonging. Maybe I had been searching for quite a while now. My father's unwillingness to see me for who I am, his inability to offer me what every kid looks for—love and acceptance—had left me always striving for more than I knew. While I had buried that man many years ago and I stopped fearing his anger even before that, his hold on me was deep.

As I walked the tangled streets and witnessed happy families breaking bread together in laughter, I found myself longing once again for a place to call home. I wished for a place to truly be myself, probably clearly realizing it for the first time in my life.

The light in the sky dimmed as I wandered street after street. In the distance, a dog barked, probably acknowledging a couple of frolicking squirrels that trespassed into his yard. Acorns crunched under my feet as I crossed the street. Families finished their suppers and cleared their tables. Soon kids ventured outside for one last romp before bedtime. Fathers tackled their sons in chase of footballs. Mothers pushed their daughters on swing sets. Distantly happy, I watched from the sidewalk these families, who played no more than ten feet from me and who were Minnesota born just like me, and I couldn't help but want for the simple joy of a place to belong. I turned the corner and made my way back to the Smith's home.

That night, Mrs. Smith and I ate alone on the porch. We chatted about the weather and politics, but mostly I shared memories of my old teacher. She seemed pleased by my stories, and I was happy to reminisce.

There was the time Mr. Smith gave us a pop quiz. It was probably the hardest quiz I had ever taken. At the end of class, after we had all finished the quiz and turned it in, he smiled at us, wished us a great rest of our day, and threw all the quizzes into the trash can.

There was the time he drove me home from a basketball game senior year. The game was particularly physical, and the referees seemed clueless to the beat-down the opposing team was inflicting upon me each time I tried to bring the ball up the court. We squeaked out a win on the road. He couldn't stop telling me how proud he was of how I'd played and how I'd handled the adversity of the game. We pulled up to the house to find my father stumbling up the front stairs.

There was the time he showed us a mathematical proof on the chalkboard. I have no clue how he got to math in our humanities class, but that was Mr. Smith. He was getting so excited. He amused the entire class, but no one found the proof all that interesting. He couldn't believe we weren't more into it, so he got more and more excited. He began waxing on about the beauty of mathematics and how powerful the proof was. Finally, he blurted out to the class, "You guys! This is better than sex!" Right at that moment Mr. Callaghan, our school headmaster, was walking by the classroom door.

Mr. Smith froze, and the entire class burst into laughter.

Mrs. Smith chuckled with each story. Her gaze was fixated off in front of her, on nothing in particular. Her smile was wistful. The warm night air persisted even after the sun dropped below the horizon. A calm breeze blew across the porch from time to time, and our conversation drifted aimlessly with the wind, which was just the way she seemed to want it. A sadness sat between us both as we talked of better times. The man we both loved lay asleep in the next room. I felt pained by the thought of this wonderful woman losing her longtime partner.

"Thank you, Mrs. Smith," I said sincerely as my stories began to wane. Our eyes met, and I can't really explain why, but I could see in her eyes everything she was feeling at that moment. Maybe it was because I was experiencing a range of mixed emotions myself. All the love she had, the gratefulness of the years with her husband, the laughter they always seemed to share, the pain that develops over the course of any relationship, and the sadness the disease had thrust upon her, all of it sat in those eyes. I reached out and squeezed her hand. She smiled, stood up and hugged me closely. Then she cleared the plates and made her way inside.

I climbed into bed, haggard from the long trip and all of the emotions I hadn't fully processed. Staring at the ceiling, I waited for sleep to come. As I finally drifted off, I worried that my dear teacher wouldn't wake in the morning.

I started awake as the sun rose outside. I wandered out of the guest room with an overwhelming sense of dread. This would probably be the last time I ever saw my old teacher, and I begged that it would be one last time alive.

A wave of relief poured over me when I stepped onto the porch. There he sat hand in hand with his wife. They both beamed when they saw me. Mrs. Smith quickly rose to her feet and again offered me her chair despite my protestations. Bagels and pastries sat on the table. The weather was overcast and dark clouds loomed in the distance.

"Help yourself, James," she said as she disappeared inside for a moment. I spread cream cheese on a bagel, and soon she emerged with a hot cup of coffee, which she handed to me. I smiled, relieved to be sitting on the porch with Mr. Smith smiling back at me.

"Maria was just informing me that you told her the story about the mathematical proof." His voice was a little softer than yesterday afternoon, his pace a little slower, but he maintained the playfulness in his tone as he looked at me accusingly. "That didn't need to be shared."

My smile grew bigger. "It didn't need to be shared, but it sure did want to be."

He chuckled. "That was a great proof, my boy. You all should have been much more excited than you were. I needed to motivate you to see things more clearly."

We both began laughing at the memory once again. "The timing couldn't have been more perfect," I said through my laughter. "Your face was priceless. You just froze when you saw the headmaster."

Mr. Smith began chuckling harder. "Mr. Callaghan was not pleased with me, explaining math to teenagers like that. I guess I got a little carried away during that lesson."

His laughter grew even more and it quickly turned into coughing. He hacked, and his face contorted as he tried to catch his breath. His wife began patting his back firmly. When the coughing subsided, he leaned back in his chair with his eyes closed. Mrs. Smith wiped spit from his chin with her napkin. She stood over her husband until his eyes finally opened. The two exchanged faint smiles, communicating something that only the two of them understood. I sat feeling guilty that I had gotten Mr. Smith so worked up.

After another minute of catching his breath, Mr. Smith looked at me smiling. "He was not happy at all."

"I'm sure reprimands were given," I chuckled cautiously.

"Sure. Sure. It wasn't the first time, and it wasn't the last. My methods weren't," he paused, "'conventional' let's say." He finished as he motioned quotes in the air.

I nodded with a smile and took a sip of coffee. Letting the caffeine do it's work, I began to shake off the sleep. Mr. Smith was staring off at nothing, his mind clearly somewhere else.

"You're not well, are you, James?" he said after a minute.

I didn't quite know how to respond. "I'm fine, Mr. Smith. I'm just glad to see you."

"I know you're fine, James. You'll always be fine. It's not in your constitution not to be fine. But you're not well."

"Really, I'm fine, sir. I'm just trying to find my way a little bit right now. It's nothing worth discussing."

"And why's that?"

Before me sat my old teacher, inching toward death, asking me why I am disillusioned by my own life, why my desire for a place to belong is not worth discussing. I wasn't sure how to answer that. I wanted to say any number of things. *Because you're dying, and I'd rather not focus on myself right now. Because people have it far worse than I do, and my problems are miniscule in comparison. Because I actually am fine. Why would I expect to be doing any better than fine?* Instead, I sat silently.

"Have I ever told you the story of how Maria and I met, James?"

I shook my head without looking in Mr. Smith's direction.

"We were young and had both recently graduated from college. I'd moved back into my parents' house for the summer, trying to figure out what I would do with my life. I had to decide what my next step would be, but I was a lost young man. I was still haunted by the death of a friend who had fallen from a cliff and I was scared of how short my life could be. I had no idea what I wanted to do next. I was considering grad school and a variety of other options. I sat at a local bar with some buddies that used to be on the other side of town. It was a frigid night, one of the coldest of the year. I saw Maria walk in with some of her friends, and I couldn't look away. I'm sure I was just gawking at her."

"He was." Mrs. Smith's eyes rolled while she simultaneously smiled.

"I knew I had to go talk to her," my old teacher continued. "I spent the next hour working up the courage. My friends slowly started to leave the bar and venture out into the cold, snowy night. Finally, I did it. I saw her approach the bar alone, and I made my move. Before I said more than five words, she turned to me and smiled that smile of hers and said, 'Not interested.'"

"Really?" I said. I was partially amused and partially surprised. "What'd you say?" I asked as I took a bite of my bagel.

"After being stunned, I gathered myself and said, 'I think you are, you just don't know it yet.' Then I turned and walked away, smoother than I had ever been in my life."

"It took months before she would agree to even go on a date with me. Finally, she did, probably because I wore her down. It took a couple years, but eventually she was interested, and she agreed to marry me."

I took a sip of coffee. "That's sweet, sir." I paused. I wanted to ask him why he was sharing this with me. What did this have to do with him asking how I was doing? Was he losing it?

"Maria has been incredible, James. She's always been my rock. We've had plenty of ups and downs. There was a rough point early in our marriage where she took a vacation by herself and I waited at home worrying that she might never come back. But I knew from the first day I met her in that bar, from that point on, my life had meaning. Maria convinced me to stop working construction and become a teacher. Maria always encouraged me to be passionate. She always expected the best out of me. She gave me purpose."

The past tense in the word "gave" sat heavy on my heart. I didn't like it, even though I understood the reality before him.

Mr. Smith sat deep in thought. His eyes were hazy, lacking focus. He breathed deeply and then looked at me, "Find meaning each day, James. Without meaning, we're lost. Without meaning, we become bored, or complacent, or depressed, or lonely. Meaning is the key to happiness." Mr. Smith's breath was more labored than it had been yesterday. He closed his eyes as if to search his brain for a lost anecdote.

"Holocaust survivor Viktor Frankl tells a story about a question posed to the world grandmaster chess champion. 'Tell me, Master, what is the best move in the world?' The world champion chuckles and explains that there is no best move. There is no one move better than all the others. There are not even good moves apart from a particular situation in a game and that particular opponent's personality.

"Frankl concludes that the same logic applies to human existence. There is no abstract meaning of life, James. Each person has his own vocation. Your life cannot be repeated, nor can it be replaced. Your purpose is unique to the specific opportunities that are presented to you and to no one else. And it's not always the same purpose throughout the course of your life, just as there is not always a best chess move throughout the course of a game. Your purpose may change, but always strive to know what that purpose is. We belong, James, simply because we are. No one can take that away from us."

I thought about Mr. Smith's comparison of life to a game of chess as my old teacher sat next to me knocking at death's door but offering me one last lesson. In this moment, life didn't seem like a game to me at all.

Mr. Smith sighed, taking a number of long, purposeful breaths before he continued. "Each of us has our struggles in life, James. Each of us has things to be sad about, or to be angry about, or to be afraid of. But there's power in our pain, my boy. It just depends on how you use it. Life is constantly presenting you with positive and negative experiences. That's just a fact of life. And they're exactly that in the moment—positive or negative. You can't control that. But after the moment, after you've had the experience, the negative and the positive are worth the exact same amount. Once you've had the experience, any experience at all, after that moment has passed, it's yours to control. You decide what that experience is worth, no one else."

Mr. Smith clutched a cup of hot water in both hands. The sky had darkened even more over the last hour. A tree in the front yard began to sway irregularly as gusts of wind blew. My old teacher's eyes fixated on the tree jerking with the passing wind, then standing motionless, then jerking once again. I watched the tree with recognition of the wonderment with which Mr. Smith now gazed at it as it fought the gusts to stand still once again.

"This has been the age-old question, James. 'What is the meaning of life?' But maybe that's exactly what Life is asking of us, and you can only answer it by answering for your own life, no one else's. You answer Life by being responsible for your own experiences, the good and the bad."

He sat silently in his chair. His eyes were closed now, and he looked content. I sipped the last of my coffee as that minute of silence stretched into ten. Mr. Smith was lost somewhere in thought. Mrs. Smith was enjoying watching her husband do what he loved best—teach. I wasn't about to break the silence, even if I had had something meaningful to say, which I hadn't. Mr. Smith's tree in his front yard gave in to the gusts of wind and began to sway effortlessly with each breeze. I sat silently try-ing to push back tears. A light rain began to fall. We watched it silently from the protection of the porch. The pitter-patter on the concrete offered a soft concerto to Mr. Smith's lesson.

"I am a happy man, James. I've had a good life. I have a wonderful wife who I love dearly. You have a world of possibilities before you, son. You have years of experiences before you and years of deci-sions to make. I no longer have possibilities, just realities. But I don't long for it to be different at all. I have the reality of the hard work I've put in. I have the love I have given. And something I may be even more proud of than anything else, I have the reality of the sufferings I encountered in life and how I bravely faced them. I don't long to be young with a future of possibilities. I'm content with the life I lived. I'm proud of my realities. I'm content that I answered Life's question—my life had meaning."

Mrs. Smith looked away as her eyes welled up. I choked back my own tears, furrowing my brow in determined consternation to keep them from welling up. Mr. Smith leaned up from the back of his chair and opened his eyes. He rested his elbow on the table and looked over to me.

"You're a good man, James. You were a wonderful boy. I loved watching you grow up. And you're a good man now. Don't forget that."

A tear fell from my eye, then a second. My old teacher stood up from his chair. Slowly, with help from his wife, he made his way to me as I stood.

"You should hit the road before the weather gets much worse. You've done well, my boy," he said. "Don't stop."

He wrapped his arms around me. The man I once knew to be so strong felt frail. I embraced my old teacher for as long as I could. Then he stepped back and smiled with all the kindness in the world.

"So long, my friend," he said.

"Thank you, Mr. Smith. I love you."

We both hugged one last time. Then his wife took his arm, and they slowly moved inside.

I fell back into my chair. The tears I had been holding back now poured out. My head rested in my hands as I brushed tears from my face. I didn't want to go. I didn't want to stay. I was numb.

I felt a soft hand on my back and looked up to see myself gazing into the loving eyes of my old teacher's doting wife. She pulled her chair directly in front of me.

"Thank you, James. You have made a dying man happier than you know. It was quite a tremendous effort for you to come here."

"Stop..." I sniffled, wiping my eyes.

"Don't reject the gratitude, James. It's true, you are incredibly kind. It means so much to me and to my husband."

She squeezed my hand tightly. "Please keep in contact, okay?"

I nodded, fighting back more tears. Mrs. Smith hugged me closely, then rose to her feet and disappeared inside. There I was, left to myself on the front porch of my beloved teacher. The rain began to fall harder. I watched the water bounce off the concrete. Each droplet hit the pavement and exploded into hundreds of fragments, unable to control the direction of the spray after impact. With fractal division, each new tiny droplet itself exploded into fragments. The rain soon poured down making each droplet indiscernible from the next, a flood of raindrops coming down in sheets.

I wiped my hazy eyes and grabbed my things from my bedroom in a daze. The door at the end of the hall was closed. The tears welled up again. I threw my bag onto my shoulder and ventured out into the storm as the water soaked me. Sitting wet and dazed in the front seat, I whispered to my wonderful teacher, "I love you." Then, I eased the car out of the driveway and began my long journey home.

DIES CUM ANXIETA

I wake up next to my beautiful wife. My amazing one year-old daughter lies just feet from me. I watch her silently while she sleeps; her cute little butt sticks up in the air while her knees scrunch up close to her chin. When she begins to stir, I rub the sleep out of my eyes. This is my favorite part of the morning.

She briefly tosses, and then pushes up into the seated position. She rubs her eyes, like I had done just moments ago. My little baby is learning from me already. I'm a proud papa watching her wake for another day of life. She looks around, confused about where she is. Her eyes are still adjusting to the dark room.

I wonder what she must be thinking. I'm sure she was enjoying a lovely dream frolicking with mom in fields of lilies. Now she's in a dark bedroom trying to get her bearings. Her eyes lock on me, and my heart skips a beat. Her eyes try to focus. She stares for what must be ten seconds. Then:

"Dada."

I beam with pride.

"Dada. Dada." She repeats.

It seems to be her favorite phrase these days, and I couldn't be more excited to hear it. I climb out of bed to pick her up before she wakes my beautiful wife, who is laying next to me. That's when my lifelong companion, the one that knew me far before I met my wife, wakes up from his slumber as well.

How is this your daughter? You're going to ruin her, you know? You'll screw it up. At some point you'll screw it up. You're no dad. Not a good one anyway.

I grab my daughter in my arms. She leans her head into my shoulder. I squeeze her tight as we slip out of the room before we wake my wife.

"Dada," she repeats. Then: "Ball. Ball."

I am a big basketball fan. I enjoy playing it, watching it, reading about it; pretty much anything basketball-related I enjoy. My daughter, in only sixteen months of life, has picked this up. She loves to say "dada" and "ball." She even mimes like she's dribbling a basketball. I'm proud.

I put some waffles into the toaster and begin slicing a banana. I refill her sippy cup with whole milk and lay the feast before her on the table as I strap her into her booster seat. She beams at me with glee.

"Nana."

"Yea!" I say excitedly. "Ba-na-nas. Wa-fuls. Milk." I point at each item in front of her as I sound them out. She lunges at a waffle and begins eating, giggling.

I start the coffee in hopes it will shake the rest of this sleepy haze from my brain.

Bananas and waffles? Really? Your wife would have made something way better. Your wife is so much better at this. How are you a parent? Your daughter probably hates that she's stuck with you.

The coffee finishes brewing, and the coffee-maker beeps. I pour myself a cup and take a sip.

"Dada. Haaahhhttt," my daughter says, pointing to the coffee cup in my hand.

My God, she is wonderful. How did she get so smart? I notice three banana slices on the floor around her. She smiles at me and then, not so innocently says, "Uh-oh."

Soon the three of us are racing around finalizing our morning routine. I hug my baby girl and give her a kiss on the forehead. I hug my wife, and we kiss for a moment before our daughter separates us. "That's my mama," her look says to me. Message received. We venture in our own directions—my wife's off to drop our daughter at daycare before heading to the company she owns and runs; mine to walk to my desk job.

Your wife thinks you're disgusting. She settled for you, ya know? You do know that, right? She barely tolerates you. Did you see that look she gave you after she kissed you?

I sit down at my desk. Clients from Europe have already been emailing throughout the night. A few clients on the east coast have left voicemails. I begin the morning routine of clearing both.

I review a contract for a client. I make a call to a party on the other side of a deal I'm negotiating. I research a few new high-tech products about to be released on the market. I begin reading a technical analysis from a consultant.

You call yourself an attorney? You're just a fake. Your parents are probably glad you live fifteen hundred miles from home. They have five other kids—the successful ones. You could disappear, and your parents wouldn't even notice.

I sit through a management meeting.

"What do you think?" my CEO asks. The team looks at me awaiting my opinion on what we should do with a high profile client. I provide my perspective as confidently as I can.

There's a short pause. Then my CEO nods in approval. "I agree. That's what we need to do." Everyone else nods along. They agree it's the best strategy.

What a stupid idea. You should hear what they're saying about you now that you've left the conference room.

They know you're a joke. Just stop pretending. You're garbage.

I look at Facebook, checking to see how some of my friends and family are doing. My youngest brother has posted an angry rant about the power of positive thinking and how it cures all ills. The irony seems to be lost on him that he presents his diatribe with such vitriol. My sister jabs at him with a witty post referring to Deepak Chopra and mindfulness. It's lost on me, but I post my own jab next to hers.

Oh. My. God. What does that even mean? Are you a moron? You're not funny. You're not even witty. Just shut up now, please.

My entire afternoon is spent on one call after another. One client needs advice on a negotiation strategy. Another client wants insight into a recent purchase by a competitor. I move seamlessly from one client issue to the next, a fire fighter of sorts. Soon the world outside my office window begins to fade to black. I pack up my things and walk the two miles back home.

My daughter hears my keys rattle in the door. She's pounding on the other side, knocking for me to let her in. She hasn't quite grasped the concept that the person on the outside is the one that should knock. When I open the door, she immediately throws her head back in delight. She giggles as she stares up to the ceiling, and then she grabs two of my fingers with her tiny hands. She leads me directly to the dining room table where my wife is just setting down dinner.

"Thanks honey," I say as I kiss my wife hello. "You're wonderful." We embrace for a moment before our daughter once again separates us.

I pour myself a glass of red wine, to which my daughter immediately points and says, "Dada." She's not pointing at me. She's pointing at the wine. Should I be concerned that she equates coffee, basketball, and red wine with me?

The three of us sit down and say grace. My wife and I converse about our respective days while we're periodically interrupted by banging, food throwing, yelping, and other various sorts of interruptions that a one-year old provides. Dinner is anything but uneventful. Soon we're clearing the table and reading books.

As I play hide and seek with my daughter, I think, *Where did the evening go?* She's in her pajamas and her teeth are brushed. This is her favorite thing to do each night before bedtime. My wife makes sure the room is otherwise prepared for the nightly slumber. My daughter slowly pulls open the closet and sees me hiding. She yelps and runs away with glee.

My beautiful daughter has finally fallen asleep. My wife and I enjoy each other's company for an hour while we watch TV. Our energy begins to fade. The long day has caught up to us. We head upstairs to climb into bed and read. I brush my teeth and change as quietly as any human has ever done so as not to wake my daughter. I slip into bed.

My wife leans over to whisper, "You're louder than a herd of elephants." She smiles and kisses me on the shoulder.

I periodically glance over at her as I read. She's slowly fading off to sleep. I smile and can't help but think how lucky I am. My old friend seems to agree.

How does one man get so lucky? You don't deserve any of this you, worthless waste of space. You are essentially disgusting and a loser. Soon everyone you love will leave you, and that's what you deserve.

I roll over to switch off the light. My pillow wraps itself around my weary head. I close my eyes and hope he'll be quiet long enough for me to fall asleep.

THE SECOND SORROWFUL MYSTERY:

FATHER

He awoke with little trouble on this cold October morning. In truth, he rarely struggled to rise. This morning was no different insofar as he was able to quickly wake from his slumber; although on this particular morning, he rolled out of bed fifteen minutes later than usual.

When his alarm finally snapped him from his dreams and to the attention of the waking world, he knew that almost everyone else in the city was still asleep. Despite stealing fifteen extra minutes, the time on his bedside clock shared that it was 4:45 A.M.

He rubbed his eyes gently as he swung his feet over the side of the bed. Other than the dim red light from his alarm clock, the room was pitch black. He shuffled slowly to the bathroom running his bare feet along the plush gray carpet. He loved the feel of the soft carpet on his feet as he dragged his arches along the floor. It was his odd ritual. Every morning when he rolled out of bed, he would slowly shuffle across the carpeted floor; the rest of his body was urged awake from his sleepiness as the carpet sent quiet sensations from his feet throughout his body. He flipped on the bathroom light and let the hot shower run until it was warm.

Michael Birch grew up in the heart of the northern Midwest. As a young boy, he and his two brothers loved the fall months. The way the weather transitioned from the scorching and humid summers to the unforgiving frigid winters left the world painted with vibrant fall colors, if even for a brief moment in time. The trees on the street on which they grew up would reverberate with undeniably pulchritudinous color. As a kid he remembered wondering why these colors were never anywhere else except on the trees for a short stretch of time at the end of September and beginning of October.

The yellows, reds and oranges bellowed so boldly that he used to stare captivated by colors. They were simple, but the way they mixed together forming a seemingly never-ending palate of new hues amazed him. He used to imagine that each leaf had its own incontrovertible personality, some shouting with intrepid redness, others humbly waiting their turn to share their coral tone, while others still quietly donned their yellow glow. Each leaf had its place on Michael Birch's tree-lined street, and the trees welcomed all the personalities brought by each leaf.

When he was young, it was usually at this point of his gazing wondrously at the leaves above that he would be clunked with a football.

"What are you doing, you doofus!?" his brother Tom would call.

"Keep your eye on the ball!" William would chime in.

"Yea, yea," he'd reply and scurry after the bouncing football.

His older brothers were his teachers and his protectors. Tom was the oldest of the three boys. He took it upon himself to watch after his younger brothers. He was always on guard and aware of their surroundings. He felt a need to make William and Michael feel safe.

William was the middle child. He was a year and half younger than Tom and two years older than Michael. Even at a young age he had a quick wit and a sharp intellect. He intuitively grasped concepts typically difficult for a young boy, and after internalizing the new lesson, he would be sure to teach the new idea to his brothers, particularly Michael. William felt it was his duty to teach Michael everything he knew. If Michael didn't know something, William experienced it as a fault of his own, not of Michael's, so he was constantly instructing his younger brother.

The three brothers were well known throughout the St. Paul neighborhood where they grew up. "Here come the Birch Brothers," you could often hear the neighbors sigh, sometimes in admiration, but most often in abject concern for the mischief the boys were getting into. While they were well-meaning children, the saying that boys-will-be-boys was well-fitting for the Birch Brothers.

It was still dark when Michael walked across the street from his house to the rectory. He checked his watch, six A.M. exactly. He had finished his morning prayers after showering and read his daily scriptures over coffee. He pulled his wool sweater tighter around his neck as the cold fall wind bade him good morning. He smiled as a breeze sent a jolt throughout his system. He loved fall today as much as he had when he was a boy.

He loved the reprieve that fall brought after the Minnesota summers. There was something he loved about putting on a sweater for the first time at the coming of fall and sitting outside in the brisk air with a cup of coffee. The fall air always smelled fresher than it did the rest of the year. A sweet scent would hang in his nose during those crisp fall days.

Each breath, as he crossed the street, awakened his mind with the gentle hint of cold, but calmed his soul with the peacefulness that fall brings. He listened to the crunch of leaves under his feet with each step—a sign that everything beautiful will fade and everything living will someday die. Most men would find this type of thought to be morbid and morose, but Michael did not. He found the tenuous nature of human existence to be calming.

As he approached the rectory, he grabbed the keys from his pocket and unlocked the door. As was customary, he was the first to enter the building that morning. He turned up the heat and went through his normal routine preparing for 7:00 AM daily Mass.

Michael had been a priest for nearly fifteen years now. When he and his brothers entered their teenage years, Tom and William naturally took to daydreaming about their female classmates. They dated frequently throughout their teenage years and into their twenties. Michael, on the other hand, found the flirtatious quality of their intermittent relationships to be young folly. It's not that he knew at a young age that he wanted to be a priest, but rather that he knew he didn't want to date often and frequently. Then, around the age of twenty-five, he decided he would try the seminary.

His brothers supported him in his decision but often joked that he would soon fail out. "We Birch boys like girls too much," they'd chide.

Little did they understand that Michael did not share the same romantic outlook the two of them had for women. It wasn't until the end of his priestly schooling that Michael knew he was called to be a priest. While in the seminary, his older brothers had found themselves wives and started their own families. And so it came to pass that the Birch Brothers became the Birch Fathers—Tom and William falling in love and raising children of their own, and Michael becoming a Catholic priest.

Michael said Mass that morning with little fanfare. The front pews were scattered with a few dozen regulars, while one or two new faces sat in the middle of the church. Michael had now been pastor for nearly six years. It was one of the largest churches in the Twin Cities. Over a thousand families called his church home, and many of the families were no strangers to money either. The grade school had eight hundred children and produced many talented athletes for the local high schools over the years. Michael loved guiding his large flock.

He walked through the rectory after Mass removing his vestment and grabbing his jacket.

"Don't forget, Father Michael, you have a lunch meeting with the principal of the school at noon," his rectory assistant told him as he passed.

"And good morning to you too, Gladys," Michael smiled.

She feigned a smile for a moment and then her serious tone returned. "You forgot the last meeting. Don't forget it this time."

"I won't!" he called as he scooped up his keys and walked out the front door of the rectory. As was his custom twice a week, Michael jumped into his car to visit the Miller family.

Paul and Alyssa Miller were long time members of the parish. They had two boys, both at the grade school. Sam was in seventh grade and had been altar boy for three years. He was an impressive athlete—the starting running back of the school's Pop

Warner football team and the point guard on the basketball team. Sean was two years younger and had just begun as an altar boy this year. He played soccer and basketball as well, but he found much more joy in his classes than he did his sports.

Michael had been visiting the boys twice a week for nearly a year now after their father found himself in a bit of trouble. Paul had made the family a considerable amount of money as an intellectual property attorney over the years, but he made a considerable amount more in the buying and selling of stock. Paul had bought quite a bit of Comcast shares right at the point the stock had touched its lowest in nearly five years. A few months later, he sold it all right back as the stock shot up to a six-month peak. Paul told his wealthy friends that he was tracking Comcast's patent litigation with Time Warner Cable and had made educated bets on how the litigation would affect the stock price. His knowledge of intellectual property law and patents made this plausible.

Someone at the SEC, however, found Paul's timing curious. After receiving an anonymous tip, the SEC began digging into Paul's trading patterns. The SEC eventually found that Paul had received inside information from a client. This is what allowed Paul to time the market perfectly, not the patent litigation. As it turned out, this wasn't the first time he had pulled this stunt either. He had done this five other times over the years. He would take inside information on major litigation settlements and trade large amounts of stock before the public knew the information.

Paul always told himself it was just a gray area of the law, and he wasn't doing anything wrong. "If not me, someone else would do it. Why shouldn't my family benefit?" he would say.

The government didn't find it to be much of a gray area. The SEC slapped Paul with a hefty $1,750,000 dollar fine and a three-year prison sentence. The fine forced the Millers, who were overleveraged in their two houses and other investments, to sell both houses and substantially downsize their lifestyle. The prison sentence left the boys without a father during formative years of their childhood.

Michael went to visit Paul in prison soon after he arrived there nearly nine months ago. This wasn't the first parishioner Michael had visited in prison, and although he hoped it would be his last, he knew better. "Poor judgment and tragedy can befall us all," Michael would always say. Some of the guards knew Michael from around town and greeted him warmly as he checked in.

Paul was heartbroken waiting in the visitor's area. "Can you believe this?" Paul asked as Michael hugged him. Inmates were allowed to touch visitors twice each visit—once when they arrived and once when they left.

Paul and Michael sat across from each other at a small table. "This is quite a turn, Paul," Michael nodded. "God always has a plan, though. Remember to accept your part in what brought you to this point. Look for any silver linings while you're in this situation."

"What silver linings?"

"I'm not sure. That will hopefully be revealed to you in due time."

"My part in this," Paul sneered. "There are criminals raping and murdering people out there, and I'm stuck in here. For what? All because I helped my family and my parish earn some money. Some justice."

Michael smiled back kindly. "Just make the most of it," he said. What he was thinking was something completely different. He wanted to say, "You have a long road ahead of you with your current attitude," but he thought there would be plenty of time for that during other visits.

"Father Michael," Paul said with an urgent concern in his voice. He reached across the table and grabbed the priest's hand.

"Inmate!" yelled a guard at the door. "No touching!"

Paul's hand quickly retreated. His fingers began tracing lines in the wooden table. His eyes glazed over while he stared downward.

"My boys," his voice was lower and strained. Michael could tell Paul wanted to cry, but he wouldn't let himself. He knew not to show weakness in prison, especially not this early in his sentence.

"I will," Michael assured him.

Paul raised his eyes and met Michael's kind gaze from across the table. "Make sure they're okay, Father Michael. Please. Take care of them for me, okay?"

"I will, Paul. They're good boys. They're going to be okay."

"Thanks." Paul nodded still trying to withhold tears.

Instinctively, both men stood and embraced one more time. "I'll be back in a couple weeks," the faithful priest assured. "Remember to look inward," he said while pointing a finger to Paul's chest, "and remember to look upward."

....

After 7:00 A.M. mass, Michael drove a few miles up the interstate. Alyssa and the boys were now renting a modest home on the other side of the city. After selling the homes and removing much of the excess from their lives, they found they couldn't afford to live in the same neighborhood anymore, so they moved across town and rented. Without Paul's salary to count on, buying was out of the question.

Michael knocked at the front door, pulling his jacket tight as the wind whipped across the priest's face. Alyssa smiled as she opened the door.

"Come in, Father Michael," she greeted.

Sean and Sam were sitting at the kitchen table eating breakfast. They both looked up and smiled.

"Hi, Father Michael!" Sam beamed.

"Hi, Sam," Father smiled back.

Sean reached his hand out for a fist bump, to which Michael responded in kind. Sean retracted his hand from a balled fist to a downward facing palm while he made an explosion noise. Both he and Sam laughed.

Michael pulled up a chair to the table.

"How's school going, Sean?"

"Good!" Sean's exuberance surpassed that which is typically expressed by the average fifth grade male. "Mom and I are working on a project for the Science Fair. We're testing mouthwash and how good it is at killing germs!"

"Really? That sounds fascinating. How are you doing that?" Michael leaned up to the table to show his interest.

"We got petri dishes! Yep, and we took...ummm...mom?" Sean looked at his mother who poked her head in from the other room.

"Bacterial cultures."

"Yep, I knew that," Sean beamed. "Bacteria cultures. We used cotton swabs to get multiple ones from Mom, Sam, and me. There are nine in all. I wanted to get one from Dad too, but Mom said they wouldn't let me." Sean's eyes moved downward toward the table.

Michael sensed the boy's sadness. He gave Sean a chipper response to pick him up. "That sounds incredible, Sean! It sounds like something for someone far smarter than myself. I'm glad someone with your brains is tackling that science project."

Sean's eyes looked back up, and his excitement slowly returned. "It should be really cool," the boy replied.

"It is. Make sure to let me know which mouth-wash works the best so I can purchase accordingly in the future."

"Ok!" Sean bounded away from the table. "Mom, I'm done with breakfast. I'm going to check on the petri dishes," he called as he ran to his bedroom.

Alyssa gave her approval as she called from the other room. She had been shuffling and filing papers since Michael entered their house. There were always bills to pay and the boys' school papers to check.

"And how about you, Sam?" Michael turned to Sean's older brother who was reading the back of the cereal box.

"I'm fine," Sam replied casually looking up from the box. "I ran for two touchdowns last Saturday in our game."

"I heard, Son. That is impressive, especially against mostly eighth graders. You seem to be getting better each week." Sam smiled at the compliment. Michael knew these boys starved for that fatherly approval while their dad was in prison. He tried to encourage them every opportunity he had.

"And what about school?" Michael continued.

"Meh. It's school, Father Michael. That's Sean's thing."

"It's every bit your thing too, Sam. You're just as smart and capable in the classroom as you are on the football field. You know, when I was your age..."

"Oh man. Not another story, Father Michael," Sam groaned. He stood up from the breakfast table and placed his bowl in the dishwasher.

"No no, Son. I won't bore you with something as trivial as Father Michael's life," the good priest replied sarcastically. "Just don't dismiss your class-work. Okay? You're really good in your classes. They're important. Keep up the good work."

"I know, I know," Sam moaned as he wandered off to his bedroom.

Alyssa walked into the kitchen. "Five minutes and Father Michael has to leave boys," she called to her sons who were nowhere in sight. A mother's voice can reach all corners of the home.

"Can I get you a cup of coffee, Father Michael?" she asked in a much softer tone.

"No, no thank you. I am well caffeinated for the morning." Michael paused for a moment. "How are you, Alyssa?" Michael was always very careful to keep a respectful distance from Alyssa and her own personal struggles. He was careful with all of his parishioners. But he wanted to make sure they all knew the door was open. He wanted them to know that his kind ear was always nearby.

"I'm okay, considering. Thank you for asking, Father."

"Remember to take time for yourself. I know that's easier said than done, but it's important, for both you and your boys. Don't forget to talk to God."

Alyssa just smiled as she wiped down counters and swept the kitchen floor.

"I'm not preaching," Michael continued, "just speaking from experience. God's always there to listen."

"I know, Father. Thank you." Alyssa stopped sweeping for a moment and looked across the kitchen at her parish priest. "For everything."

The boys bounded out of their bedrooms with their backpacks strapped around their shoulders. Alyssa would soon be heading across town to her administrative job, but first she had to see her two sons off to school. She handed each of them a brown paper lunch sack and gave each a kiss good-bye. Sam quickly wiped his cheek clean for fear the remnants of his mother's kiss may still be there on his face when he arrived at school and saw his friends. Sean, on the other hand, leaned in close for an extra hug.

"I love you boys," Alyssa cooed as her sons marched out the door with their school priest. They waved back passively. They were soon jumping on each other's backs in the front yard.

"Bye, Alyssa," Michael waved as he followed the boys outside.

"Bye, Father," Alyssa softly said as she closed the front door behind him.

Sam had Sean on his back in the grass in the front lawn. His lunch bag was underneath him crushed, which caused Sean to yell at his brother. Michael quickly marched over to pick Sean up and brush the grass off his backpack.

"C'mon now, boys," Michael said trying to calm them both down. "Hop in the car."

As the three of them piled into Michael's car, he looked up to see the Millers' neighbor peering out her front window. Michael nodded politely and waved in her direction. The elderly woman furrowed her brow and quickly pulled the curtain shut. Michael shrugged and climbed into the driver's seat.

They drove across town back to the school. Thanking their priest, Sam and Sean ran off to play on the playground in the cold air before the bell rang. Michael hoped their dad would return to his sons soon. He thought about his own father as he watched Sam and Sean run across the playground. When Michael was too young to remember, his mother asked his father to run out to the corner store down the street to grab more milk. His old man barked something about waiting until halftime of the basketball game on TV.

A few minutes later, he grumbled something to his wife and walked to the front door. He called Tom and William, who were upstairs throwing a stuffed football as they took turns diving into their bunk beds, choreographing touchdown grabs. The boys had learned to come immediately when their father called them, and they scurried downstairs shoving each other as they ran. Two-year old Michael sat on the kitchen floor banging some pans while his mother cooked.

"Boys," their father crouched down to say as the two eldest stared up at him, "I'm going out for milk and cigarettes. I love you. Take care of your younger brother." Then he left.

They never saw their father again. Rumors had circulated that he died many years later in a car accident, but they were just rumors. In actuality, the Birch Brothers never knew why their father left that day, and they really didn't care why he left. They just knew that he left.

Michael tried to bring it up one day when he was five or six. He was working on a puzzle with William on the bedroom floor.

"I don't have any memories of dad," he said matter-of-factly without looking up from the piece he was holding.

"Probably better that you don't," William responded without looking up either.

"Why do you think he left?" Michael said, finally looking towards his brother.

"Don't give a damn," William replied coldly. "He left, and we're better off."

Michael asked William to tell him again about their father's last words to them. Michael always analyzed those words closely for hidden clues, as if the reason to why his father left and where he might have gone were somewhere hidden in those words.

"Don't you miss him?" Michael asked when William had finished.

"No," William responded brusquely.

"But maybe mom wouldn't be so sad if dad were still here."

It was at that moment that Tom walked in and overheard his younger brothers. Tom's eyes narrowed and he stared down at them, emotionless.

"Dad was an asshole. That's all you need to know about him. He left because he's a sorry excuse for a man. He didn't love me, he didn't love William, and he sure as hell didn't love you, Michael."

Then Tom's gaze turned directly towards William. "I don't want to ever catch you two speaking of that man again. He's nothing to us. We have each other, and we have Mom. That's all we need. We stick together."

William nodded his understanding, and Michael followed suit. Tom then grabbed his brothers' hands and brought them downstairs for lunch.

That was the last the three of them ever spoke of their father. Michael had thought about him infrequently, but his mind would drift to the old man from time to time. Usually it was a passing thought, wondering what tortured his father so much that he felt compelled to abandon his wife and three young boys all under the age of six at the time. Now that they were all grown and his brothers had children of their own—Tom had two sons and a daughter and William had two girls himself—the Birch brothers were determined to be better fathers than their own dad had ever been.

As Michael parked the car and dutifully marched through school administrator meetings, counseling sessions with parishioners, quiet times of prayer, and phone calls, he found himself periodically thinking of the father he never knew. His mind wandered to the anger his older brother William had shown that day when he told them never to speak of their father again. Michael had never held that level of anger toward their dad. He was mostly confused. He had so many questions that would never be answered.

Soon it was midnight, and Michael couldn't stave off sleep any longer. He climbed into bed to get a solid four hours of sleep before starting his routine again. Waking well before another soul stirred from his slumber, Michael went through his prayers and morning routine like any other day. As he removed his cassock after the 7:00 A.M. Mass, though, Michael found visitors waiting in the rectory for him.

"Father Michael?" one of the visitors inquired.

"Yes, Sir. What can I do for you?" Michael replied, extending his hand in greeting as the two police officers in his rectory quickly displayed their badges.

....

The next few days were a whirlwind. Michael found himself alternating between feelings of humility to anger to confusion to indignation to concern, all at a very rapid pace. He couldn't get his bearings, as if the ground beneath him was shifting constantly. Each new feeling brought on an onslaught of additional new emotions.

When he entered the rectory after the morning Mass, the two police officers waiting for him calmly explained that they had received some calls from concerned citizens. In dazed confusion, not quite understanding the severity of the situation at first, Michael's mind raced to try to think of which parishioner of his was involved. He quickly filtered through which individuals from his parish had shown signs of anger or a capacity to abuse their families, remembering the ones that he had made a mental note to keep an eye on in the future.

It wasn't until one of the officers explained that with the times being what they were, they had to take all accusations against Catholic priests very seriously. They had opened a file to log the complaints. One citizen in particular was quite concerned with how much time he spent at the Millers' house. She had called multiple times over the last few months.

As Michael began to realize that the police were actually there for him, the rapidly changing emotions began, and they didn't stop all day. When he asked the officers if he was under arrest, they assured him that he was not. They did recommend, though, that he come down to the station on his own accord. They wanted to protect everyone involved until they could decide if they would open an official investigation or not, and they were hoping to do so without commotion from the press and community.

Unfortunately for Michael, someone soon leaked that the pastor at a local Catholic Church was down at the police station. Michael spent nearly two hours with the officers answering any questions they had. They were very appreciative of Michael's willingness to speak with them. By the time Michael grabbed his jacket to leave the station, an eager young photographer was outside ready to take the scandalous picture, and it was the perfect picture too.

In the foreground was Father Michael buttoning the top button of his black jacket. In the still frame it looked as if an embarrassed priest were trying to hide his white clerical collar from sight. Michael's head was ducking into his jacket to avoid the cold wind, but it came across in the photo as someone hiding. In front of Michael were two police cruisers parked in ominous fashion. Above his head the building read "St. Paul Police Department" in bright white letters. In the background were the two cops that had asked him to come down to the station, both with faces scrunched up from the wind, leaving them with a freeze frame of perfect scowls.

If pictures are worth a thousand words, this picture said it all: another priest is a terrible abuser. It didn't take long before the young man had sold his photograph to the local paper, which quickly scooped that the Millers' neighbor was the primary accuser. When the journalist went to her house that afternoon, she found an elderly woman eager to offer quotes implying salacious detail. The story first appeared on the paper's website in the late afternoon. The article was quick to point out that all abuse was alleged, that the police had not arrested the local priest, and that no charges had even been filed against him. That mattered little, though. With the current religious climate, all anyone needed was the photograph and the headline to reach their own conclusions without knowing more: "Local Priest Investigated for Abuse."

Soon the local television stations were pulling block quotes from the neighbor to show on their nightly news.

"It's about time someone puts a stop to this."

"Enough is enough."

"He disgusts me."

The photograph of Michael leaving the police station was shown again and again. Newscasts pulled recent statistics of abuse by Catholic priests and referenced other horrible incidents of abuse from around the nation. One station went to get their own quote from the neighbor, only to notice the Miller boys were just streaming from their mother's car into the house. The cameraman quickly got the footage he needed of the victims, without concern for the children's well-being or that everything was merely alleged.

Michael didn't know what hit him. One of the national news outlets ran a one-sentence blurb on their bottom line during the morning show the next day. Soon the local police and government officials were overwhelmed with calls from concerned and angry citizens, who, when they learned that no arrest had been made, were furious. Phone calls flooded their lines. Local radio stations received call after call of listeners expressing outrage. Not wanting to be on the wrong side of the growing endemic of abuse by priests, the mayor and the chief of police were quick to react. Despite objections, particularly from the two police officers who'd brought Michael in for questioning the day before, they demanded an arrest to be made to assuage public concerns. They reasoned that if Father Michael was innocent, everything would be quickly resolved and all would be well.

So Michael soon found himself back in front of the police; this time they began reading his rights. Despite the officers' best efforts to be discrete, everything was documented. Another photo was taken as Michael exited the police vehicle at the back of the station. This time it was a grainy, dark photograph taken on a cell phone. That picture soon accompanied the first shot along with others that reporters were able to dig up. Stories circulated about Paul Miller's criminal activity and how Michael positioned himself to take advantage of a family in desperate need of help. There were no accusations too outlandish for the comment sections of the online local news sites.

It wasn't long, however, before the public outrage cooled off. Things unraveled as quickly as they began. Within a day the police found they had absolutely no evidence of abuse or criminal activity. The Miller boys were quick to defend the priest, as were Alyssa and Paul Miller. All indications were that Father Michael Birch was an outstanding citizen and a priest worthy of the title. Despite best efforts to dig up dirt—and between news organizations reaping the rewards of the scandalous content and the mayor's office desperately trying to avoid the embarrassment of arresting an innocent priest, significant effort was expended to try and dig up dirt—they were unable to find anything.

After keeping Michael two nights, it was clear they had to release him and drop charges. Michael's brothers used what friends and influence they had to put pressure on the other side. Michael's parish included a number of wealthy and powerful people in the local community. While not all members of the parish were in support of their pastor during the few short days of turmoil, many were, and those with influence used it. The local officials found themselves caught between an angry mob on a witch-hunt and people of influence pressing for Michael to be exonerated. With nothing to show to support the arrest, the police chief was left with little choice. They quickly backed away from the situation, pointing the blame of the errant arrest wherever else they could, but the damage was done for Michael.

The Birch Brothers were furious. They couldn't believe such a quick arrest and release would happen, especially one that was so public. Tom tried to be there for Michael as best he could. He was instrumental in getting powerful parishioners to act quickly on Michael's behalf. William, on the other hand, stewed at the beginning of the week mostly in silence. His anger was apparent to anyone who knew him. As the week progressed, however, he tried to speak publicly to anyone who would listen to him talk about the injustice, but most local media had moved on. The story was news when it was another story of outrage and abuse. When it became clear that it wasn't, no one really cared. The Birch Brothers found themselves helpless and angry.

"How soon are they going to release you?" Tom asked as the three sat in the visiting room.

"The police chief said he would be making a formal announcement soon, and they would be letting me go by the end of the day."

"Why are we even still here?" William asked. "Don't they have to let you go right away when they don't have something?" His anger was visible.

"They have 48 hours, I think," Tom chimed in.

"Yea, I think that's right," Michael concurred. "I'm trying to be cooperative and let them clean up their mess the way that they think they need to."

"Why the hell would you do that?" William was clearly venting his pent up frustrations. "They haven't done one thing for you. You shouldn't care to be cooperative at all. You should say 'F- You' and 'Let Me Go.' Why did you come in and answer questions at the beginning of the week anyway?"

"I was asked to come answer questions and make this easier for them, William. I've been more than willing to do so. Why wouldn't I be? If those boys are in trouble, I want to make sure I'm not hindering them from receiving the help they need in any way at all."

"Trouble from what?" William derisively responded.

Tom interjected trying to diffuse the rising emotions. "How have you been keeping up, Michael?"

"I'm okay. I could use a little sleep. I don't think I've really slept all week. But I'm okay otherwise."

William's fingers fidgeted along the table. He traced the edge and then folded his hands together. Then he repeated the process all over again. The circumstances were clearly causing him discomfort.

Michael looked at his brother with concern. "What's wrong?"

"Trouble from what?" William's tone was much more defeated this time. He felt helpless to protect his younger brother.

"Things aren't always right or wrong, William. It's not always black or white. Good intentions can turn out poorly."

William turned away in disgust. "Don't preach to me, Michael. I'm not interested in hearing your sermon. I want you to fight!"

"I'm not preaching. I'm trying to help you understand why I cooperated with the police and why I haven't spoken out aggressively. Those boys have a father in prison. If anyone knows how difficult, how devastating, it can be to have an absent father, it's us."

"But that's the entire point, Michael!" William was getting more agitated again. The officer standing nearby was beginning to get visibly uncomfortable and wondering if he should intervene before an altercation occurred. "Their father is in prison! You took on the burden to be there for them. You didn't have to do that, and now you're blamed for that?"

Michael slowed down his breathing as if by instinct. He spoke very softly and gently. "Those boys are without a father. Yes, I promised to help them through this difficult year. I was asked to help, but it was my choice. No one forced me. If that neighbor saw potential danger in my presence among the family, then at the very least, I can examine that possibility internally and with the authorities."

"That's a load of crap." William wasn't backing down on this. "That neighbor was nosy and inventing ghosts where there were none. She was bigoted towards you because you're a priest."

Michael paused for long moment. He looked over to Tom, who returned his gaze. Tom's eyes looked sad, but he didn't say a word. Michael folded his hands onto his lap. He looked back at William.

"Maybe she is bigoted towards priests, William, but who am I to judge that? She thought those boys were in danger, and so she called the police. Maybe they are in danger, not of a horrible crime, but maybe those boys actually need their father, not a stand-in for a year. Maybe Paul's request for me to look after his boys wasn't what was best. Maybe how closely I looked after them and cared for them, maybe it was too close. They're not my boys. It's not always black and white, William."

"Michael." Tom finally spoke, interjecting in the middle of Michael's dialogue. He looked at his youngest brother with concern. "Maybe William is right. Shouldn't we be fighting this harder? We should be out there publicly clearing your name."

"That's for another time, you guys. The first goal here is to make sure that family is okay. Their neighbor called for her own reasons. I'm not going to guess why she did it and whether she's biased towards priests. But I'm also not going to pretend the Catholic Church hasn't had a horrible recent history of neglect and child abuse. I don't regret how much I cared for those boys or how closely I looked out for their well-being; but I also don't object to someone wondering if that's too close. It's the unfortunate reality that the church has brought upon itself. It's the sad truth."

Michael closed his eyes deep in thought. "Everything happens for a reason."

"That's a bunch of shit," William yelled out. The officer motioned asking the brothers to calm down. Michael and Tom nodded apologetically while William ignored him completely. "Things don't happen for a reason. They just happen! And you're just sitting here passively letting them happen to you."

"Gentlemen," the officer approached them, "please keep it down. I don't want to have to break this up, but you're making me uncomfortable with how aggressive you're getting."

"Sorry, officer," Tom nodded. The young man moved back to his post at the door.

Michael spoke softly, "I agree, William, things just happen. There's no rhyme or reason to what happens. What happens to us is not black or white, good or bad, right or wrong. It's just not the way things are. But how we react to what happens to us does have a reason; how we receive and respond to what happens does have a purpose. We give reason to what happens through our own actions. Our response is what gives things purpose.

"I'm not sitting here passively. I've been very deliberate and thoughtful throughout this entire process. Those boys and their family are most important. What people think of me as a person and as a priest comes second."

"But what if how they think of you ends your ability to be a priest anymore? What if you can no longer be a pastor? Imagine how many more families, how many more young boys who need a strong male role model will be missing out." William's voice was now quieter, but still very agitated.

"Maybe there will be lots," Michael sighed. "Or maybe not. I'm not going to guess at that. All I can do is take the best actions I can in the interest of those boys and that family. If that somehow allows the press or other people to paint me in a guilty light, I'm not concerned. What they think of me is merely my reputation."

"But your reputation can dictate whether you remain pastor or not," William pressed on.

"True, but it's only my reputation and it's only who they think I am. My character is who I really am. I'm taking the best actions I think I can at this point. If acting rightly hurts my reputation, then so be it. I don't want a stalwart reputation if it requires me to go against my conscience. I want to take actions that strengthen my character, and actions that strengthen the character of those around me."

The three brothers grew silent. They just sat with each other without saying a word for a matter of minutes.

It was Tom who stood up first. "I love you," he said as he hugged Michael. The guard considered breaking up the hug but decided against it.

"I love you too."

Then Tom grabbed William's hand and raised him to his feet. The two oldest brothers embraced.

William turned to Michael. "I love you, William," Michael said as he extended his arms.

"I love you too. I'm sorry this is happening to you."

"Happening to us," Michael replied as the two youngest brothers hugged. "This has you wrapped up as much as me. I'm sorry this is happening to you too. Thank you for walking through this with me."

"I wish you weren't always so good at deflecting," William smiled. The brothers stepped back, and both the older brothers' eyes were fighting back tears.

"You call it deflecting, the rest of the world calls it humility," Michael teased.

"Is it humility if you're pointing it out?" William teased back.

William and Michael hugged one more time. "I'll be out of here in a matter of hours," Michael called as the two older brothers left.

....

If that first week was a whirlwind, the next two months were anything but. Michael hoped things would slowly go back to normal, but when he walked out of jail after being arrested, he quickly discovered there was going to be a new normal. It began with side-glances from parishioners or teachers showing more nervousness than usual when he walked through the school. Before the ordeal, Michael had had too many invites to family dinners, fund raisers, or weekend trips to a cabin than he could possibly attend. In the weeks after his arrest and release, those invites were rare.

Michael hoped time would heal the damage that was done, but as the days wore on and things did not go back to normal, he became more and more concerned. He received the final nail in the coffin about a month after his release. It was clear his life had been permanently changed.

Michael was preparing to leave for his regular visit to Paul Miller in prison. Paul had apologized effusively for what had happened to Michael, to which the priest always assured him it was okay. As he was gathering his things in the rectory to make the drive out to the prison, Michael heard a knock on the door. The man standing in front of him introduced himself as an assistant of the archbishop, who was one of Michael's many bosses.

"The archbishop would like to meet with you in his office," the man said. "Is now convenient?"

"I guess," Michael responded hesitantly. "Can I inquire what about?"

"The archbishop will tell you," was all the man said as he motioned for Michael to follow him.

Michael followed the man into the black sedan parked out behind the rectory. The man drove ten minutes across town in silence. For the entire drive, Michael's thoughts raced on what this meeting could possibly be about. He vacillated between fear of why he was being summoned to self-assurance that it could only be a positive meeting. After hearing very little from his superiors over the last month, an impromptu meeting with the archbishop was a surprise. As he exited the car for the central offices of the archdiocese, Michael was overwhelmed with a sense of dread. The Cathedral of St. Paul loomed behind him in all its grandeur. One of the tallest churches in the U.S. overlooked Michael as he slowly made his way up the front walk.

"Thank you for coming to see me on such short notice, Father Birch," the archbishop said as Michael bowed towards him and kissed his ring. Michael took a seat. The archbishop sat behind a massive desk filled with ancient-looking books and countless documents. In the far corner of the desk was a large computer display, which cast a harsh white light.

"Of course, Your Grace." Michael's mind was racing, his eyes darting around the room trying to find some clue to the purpose of this meeting.

"How are you holding up, Father Birch? It has been quite a trying time, has it not?"

"Yes, Your Grace, but I am okay."

"That is good to hear. You look tired."

"I am tired." Michael wanted to get on with the meeting to know why he was here, but he knew patience was important right now, so he continued. "While sleep has been fleeting in recent weeks, I have focused my waking energy on my parish. There are plenty in my flock who are in need and in pain. I have taken to thinking about their troubles and praying for each of them throughout the night."

"Hmmm," the archbishop responded without really approving or disapproving. "I am sure you are wondering why I have brought you here."

Michael nodded almost imperceptibly, but said nothing. He wanted to scream yes. He wanted to ask why the archdiocese hadn't put out a public statement in support of him. He wanted to say how alone he had felt having no one from the archbishop's office reach out to him in the past month to make sure he was doing all right. He wanted to curse the entire ordeal and bemoan the lack of guidance he had received. But he said nothing.

The archbishop leaned back in his chair. "These are difficult times, Father Birch. The church is under intense scrutiny. The good and the hope we have brought to the world have become secondary during a time of so many priest abuse cases. It is a world we created for ourselves, and we are receiving our penance. There is plenty of suffering in the world, and I would say the pope is very sensitive to all kinds of suffering, but he has sent a direct message on this type of suffering. These kinds of cases will not be tolerated."

Michael shifted in his chair. He found it difficult to breathe as the air around him grew hot. The archbishop continued.

"We must bring all cases into the light. The church spent far too long hiding instances of abuse in a severely misguided and horrific aim to protect at the very time when those we are called to protect were not safeguarded. We must bring all things into the light. The sexual abuse scandals are a grave problem. Just one case of a priest abusing a minor would be enough to justify changing the church's entire structure. One case is enough for the entire church to be ashamed of itself and to do what needs to be done."

The archbishop leaned forward again. He took a deep breath and let out a long, strained sigh. His eyes narrowed as he focused across the table at Michael. "You like those Miller boys?"

"I love them, Your Grace. I have never..." The archbishop raised his hand to stop Michael short.

"I know, Father Birch. I know." Michael's superior paused a moment before beginning again. "It is a priest's duty to care for little boys and girls in holiness. A priest is called to foster our children in their encounters with Jesus, and what some priests have done is destroy this encounter. We as a church and church leaders have collectively devastated many of those we love and those we are called to nurture in their faith.

"The current times we face are ones of intense scrutiny. There's a great concern and a realization that the church has to do something. We've spent too long not doing anything, or even worse, hiding our faults. No longer."

The archbishop stared down at a piece of paper before him. He rubbed his thumb and his forefinger across his forehead. The strain on his face was clear. Michael hadn't noticed the document sitting on the archbishop's desk before. The piles of papers scattered throughout the massive desk originally hid from Michael's view the document the archbishop was now holding. Michael couldn't see what the paper said, but he could make out the official papal seal. The dread that he felt from the moment he exited the black sedan hung over him intensely like the Cathedral looming across the street. The copper-clad dome could be seen out the window of the archbishop's office.

"Father Birch, a few weeks ago I submitted to Rome approval for you to go on a retreat. I received word last night that, as I expected it would be, this request has been approved." The archbishop picked up the one page document and held it out. Michael stood from his chair to lean across the desk and take the paper.

"This document is approval for you to take an indefinite sabbatical leave. Physical and psychological fatigue can cause discouragement in the souls of priests. An endeavor such as yours requires more time spent with the Lord Jesus to recover your strength and courage to continue your road to holiness."

Despite the dread Michael had felt, he stared at the document in disbelief. The papal seal stared back at him. "Your Grace, I don't need time..." The archbishop once again raised his hand for Michael to stop.

"It's done, Father Birch. This isn't your decision to make."

Michael remained stunned. He wanted to scream out, "I've done nothing wrong!" He wanted to break down and cry right there in front of the archbishop. He wanted to set his jaw in anger and storm right out of the office. He knew it would be useless. No one cared about Michael's defense. This was bigger than him.

"What am I supposed to do?" He could hardly muster the words to ask the question.

"The goal is to pray and reflect, but take some time to rest too. Employ this time for study, or update yourself on the sacred sciences, or explore the nuances of canonical law. The ultimate goal is for a spiritual retreat of renewal.

"I'm sure you are wondering about your parish. Steps have already been taken to select your replacement. Your parish will be well taken care of and watched over. You have served your parishioners well, but your time with the parish has run its course. God is calling you elsewhere now."

Michael's mind raced. All he ever wanted was a parish to guide and watch over. He was a leader. He spent every waking hour caring for and praying for the people in his parish. He loved them dearly. Now he was told it was being taken away. Not even that. He was told it had already been taken away. It was done. There was nothing he could do about it. He couldn't believe his church was deciding to do this to him.

The archbishop rose to his feet. "Someone will contact you soon with options for where you can spend your sabbatical. Thank you for coming in today to see me, Father Birch."

With that, Michael was ushered out of the archbishop's office. He stared in disbelief as he shuffled down the long hallway that led him out to the front door. His eyes slowly shifted between staring at his feet and staring at the pictures that lined the walls. Each archbishop in the archdiocese's history stared back at him with stern and serious gazes. As he neared the end of the hallway, Michael's eyes were drawn to a plaque that boasted a scripture passage in lavish gold lettering: "But he was wounded for our transgressions, he was bruised for our iniquities: the chastisement of our peace was upon him; and with his stripes we are healed."

He shook his head solemnly and shuffled out the front door. The harsh glare of the sun blinded him as it bounced off the cathedral dome. Michael didn't know what to do next. His life was changing in an instant. He would go to the one place he could always go when he felt alone and abandoned—his brothers. He called Tom and William; both agreed to meet immediately. Michael walked down the long sidewalk slowly. The black sedan that brought him to the meeting was nowhere in sight. The wind was brisk on this fall morning. The air was cold, and he zipped his jacket tight. Winter was coming. Michael knew that the season he loved so dearly would soon give way to cold, dark winter months.

TWO FRIENDS

A friend stopped by my home today,
In fact the friends were two.
The next arrived with great dismay,
The first was meek and true.

Ever gracious host, I welcomed them both
With a kiss told through gritted grin.
For only just one, planned ahead to come,
Unbidden the other barged in.

A warm embrace—a gift of love—
My first friend did employ.
I long for time her faithful hug,
You see, 'cause she is Joy.

Uncurbed is her laugh, quick to raise a glass

Drinking deep from the cup of life.
Each moment she'll seize with a joie de vivre,
An effervescence of delight.

Friend two walked slowly up to me,
Brow furrowed, eyes quite grim.
His heart laid bare for all to see
Each glory and all sin.

Sincere was his mien, though forlorn indeed
No regard shown for tomorrow.
His presence ill-timed, no reason nor rhyme.
I greeted my dire friend Sorrow.

For weeks I planned to welcome one,
The peace of our love shared,
But finding now that two did come
Left me quite unprepared.

"You don't call ahead," I severely said.
As I pointed from whence he came.
He simply smiled warm—grace despite my
scorn—
And he settled in just the same.

Joy hugged me close and slipped away.
"I'll return," she consoled.

Discouraged tears 'cause Sorrow stayed
Welled deep within my soul.

But Joy had arrived when happiness thrived,
While hidden deep was Sorrow's song.
For he truly knows where Sorrow must go
Is where Joy had first come and gone.

THE FIRST SORROWFUL MYSTERY:

THE BALLAD OF LOVE AND HATE

(INSPIRED BY THE AVETT BROTHERS
SONG OF THE SAME NAME)

ONE

The warm air blew across the water like a free spirit. Her toes meshed with the sand. She tilted her head back to let the sun pour across her face. Her body certainly wasn't blessed with the color of the sun's kiss, but there was no question she had been spending some time on the beach. The current routine was simple—there was none. She lay in the sun when she wanted. She floated her body into water when she grew warm. A long stroll filled her mornings and a book accompanied her afternoons. In the evenings she enjoyed as many glasses of Chardonnay as seemed to fit the moment. She oftentimes didn't even wait for the evening. There wasn't a single worry. This was the beach vacation she'd always dreamed about but could never take, and now she was in the dream. She could only smile.

As she sat allowing the sun to grace her newly bronzed skin, a small group of young college boys strolled along the water's edge. One of them couldn't bring himself to look away from her. There were plenty of young women laying out, but the young man's eyes were caught by her. She loved every time this had happened in what was now over two weeks. Her body was no longer what she thought it was when she was his age, but there was an elegance and stately beauty to it now that only a quiet, confident woman could project. At least that is what she would have liked the world to think.

In reality, there had been years of watching what went into her body, years of getting off the couch when her mind and body pleaded otherwise, years of observing herself in the mirror. If asked, she would never tell you she was beautiful. Instead she would point to this wrinkle near the crest of her lip, or that ever so slight bulge in her waistline, or this hair that no longer fell in the way she had tried to train it to fall over the years. But underneath all this insecure scrutiny, there was the confidence of knowing she could still turn a head. She sat smiling toward the waves as his eyes continued to look at her now. The young man would never have known that she knew full well his gaze was upon her. She wasn't interested in reciprocating the gawking arousal. She merely enjoyed the moment when it happened—a vindication of hard work and an acceptance of the beauty within herself.

As she sat leaning back on her hands with her head tilted toward the sun, the smile projected far beyond the beach on which she lay. The group of young college boys continued down the shore. No one would have noticed that she enjoyed the long glance she received. In fact, her smile emanated well beyond that glance, but nonetheless she enjoyed it, just like she had every other glance in the past two weeks. She stared at the blue sky, looking at nothing, as if anyone who stares into the sky above stares at anything in particular. Her designer sunglasses reflected the sun beaming down on her. Her smile reflected the relaxation of a woman whose vacation had been extended far beyond her original intentions.

In her hand she held a letter. During her weeks here, she had refused to allow herself to be entrapped by the beckoning of email or the constant checking of what everyone else was doing. She had decided she needed a break from most everything she knew. "I need a break; I need rest; I need to go and reflect," she effectually said to him when she left.

Her love for him was deep. She was on vacation, but she had to send him letters of her love. And so she wrote him a new letter every day. Some days she expressed her excitement to be free, exploring her thoughts wherever they led. Other days she beamed with love for everything around her, including him. Sometimes she expressed some of her deepest hopes and fears. Those intimate thoughts that can only be realized through a pristine moment of coherence when a light flickers on in the soul. The letter she now held would be her last. It radiated the peacefulness of the days behind her, and it exuded the hope of what she had experienced. In it she expressed the beauty of the weather that graced her trip and the magnitude of the sea on which she constantly gazed. Even more importantly, at least to her, this letter expressed the excitement she now had to come home to him. Few letters before detailed this excitement, but from this letter it was clear that she couldn't wait.

....

TWO

He walked to his truck, empty lunch pail in hand. The sun had beat down throughout the day, and its intensity wouldn't cease, even at this late hour. The truck failed to immediately start, so he turned the ignition hard and gave it some gas. When it originally started to give him problems nearly a year ago, he would flood the engine trying to make it go. He now had the dance between the engine and the gas pedal down to an art. Soon the engine was roaring, the radio was blaring a song he didn't care to hear, and the uncooled circulated air was blowing against his damp brow. He adjusted the seat so that it was nearly vertical. For some reason this eased the pain in his lower back, a pain that he had lived with longer than most knew.

Everyone has pains, he'd always thought. *What's more important or severe about mine?* So the seat stood vertically today. Other days the seat leaned further back than was probably safe, all to accommodate the constant pain in his back. As he pulled off the dirt onto the paved road, he reached through the trash that lay in his lunch box and grabbed the last few bites of his second sandwich left over from earlier in the day—sun-warmed ham on white bread with American cheese melted from the long day. He took a long swig of Arnold Palmer from his canteen. He loved the perfect mixture of iced tea and lemonade. This would most likely be the majority of his dinner. Maybe he would find a frozen pizza to heat up, but in all likelihood he would drift off to sleep on the couch before he realized the hunger that he felt.

The stoplights on the drive home were exceptionally kind. At the one red light that tarnished his trip, two cute young women called to him through their open window. The blond on the passenger side pulled her glasses from her smiling face and asked him where he was going. He glanced toward their car and then back to the road ahead in time to see the light turn green. He drove off without another glance. Not a word. In his younger days he might have delighted in this attention. However, he was always reminded that she was his one and only, and he was, in fact, happy for that. He had promised his heart to her. It wasn't that he was no longer aware of a glance from a beautiful woman; it was more that he didn't seem to care any longer.

He steered his truck into the driveway and let the engine idle for a moment before shutting it down. On his way through the front door, he grabbed the mail. Setting his things down, he flipped through the contents without taking a seat. His eyebrows creased at a few bills and a solicitation for improved lawn care. Then he saw the letter, and the corners of his mouth curled upward. A peaceful excitement washed over him. He held the letter up to his face before opening it. Then he tore it. She always hated how he opened envelopes, as if he was a five year old on Christmas morning. She loved to instruct how he could more delicately create an opening. "It's going in the trash anyway," he would say. "What's the point?" This letter was nearly torn open before he paused. He took a deep breath, and with an odd frown, he gently tore the last corner. His furrowed look turned into deep concern as he began to read.

His soft blue eyes glanced left to right. He wiped some dirt off his face and then smeared his hand on his blue jeans. As he read, he walked to the fridge and grabbed a beer. It opened with a crackling mist, and he ran the can gently across his forehead. Then he took his first sip. This was the best part of his day. After a deep, pained breath, he took another sip. And another. His eyes welled up for a moment as he finished reading before his concerned look slowly contorted into a scowl. He put the letter onto the counter and took a long drink from the can. He glanced at the clock, not really caring what time it actually read. Then, without putting the can down, his first beer was finished. The empty can found a resting spot on top of the discarded letter as he went to the fridge again. Then he made his way out to the front porch.

As daylight shifted to twilight, he couldn't help but glance around the porch. He remembered stripping the six columns that held up the porch roof above. When they had first moved in, the porch was at least fifty years old, and it carried paint from all those years. He wanted to sand the porch down and put on a fresh coat of paint. She was not too happy with this idea. So, as fate would have it, he spent a summer's worth of nights stripping all the layers of paint off the porch, including each of those six columns. He removed five separate layers of paint the home's various owners had applied over the years until only bare wood remained. He had stripped it all with a handheld propane torch and a putty knife. It was a tedious process for even the most patient of individuals. Then he applied a fresh coat of primer and two fresh coats of top-end paint. He still had a small burn scar or two to show for his efforts.

The porch was now immaculate. They had received countless compliments on it over the last few years. It was a peaceful place to spend a summer evening. He hadn't had a peaceful night on that porch in a while, though. Tonight was no different. He guzzled another beer as his eyes darted from a column to the occasional passerby and then back to the column. In his younger days, he would have sat on this porch and played cards with family or strummed the guitar that he barely knew how to play. Now he simply sat. No particular care dominated his thoughts, but he sat overwhelmed with worry. This had become his ritual in recent weeks—distraught each night until fatigue cajoled him into sleep.

He carried the empty cans into the house and threw them in the trash. He glared at the clock, not seeing what it had to say. The tips of his toes curled around the threshold of the kitchen as he sighed deeply. He leaned his head back looking at the ceiling with pain-clenched eyes. When they opened, the small crack that had been growing steadily over the years stared back at him. He shook his head and leaned against the wall for a moment. "Another thing to fix," he thought. Then he shuffled across the kitchen floor, picking up the empty can left on the counter along with the letter. His eyes welled up again. *Come home*, he thought. *I am sad without you. My soul is sorrowful.* It felt like so long since they had last seen each other. He felt miserable with her away. *Or stay*, his thoughts continued, *whatever you need, I don't really care. Whatever. I've been so busy we wouldn't have been able to spend time with each other anyway. It feels like it's only been a few days because I've been so busy. I barely noticed you were gone. I'll see you soon. Or I won't. Whatever.*

He threw the can and the letter into the trash. The couch, his usual resting place these days, drew him in, and he laid his head awkwardly on the armrest. Sleep came, and another day was over.

....

THREE

Her seat shook as the plane departed from the runway. Her bronze legs stretched out before her as she gazed out the window. The yellow sundress ordained the tan she now donned with a licit beauty that every passenger had noticed when she'd boarded the plane. Her eyes followed the runway as the plane left the ground, which disappeared quickly behind her. Below her now was the sea. She smiled. The plane pierced through the sky, which was speckled with a few clouds but otherwise remained a clear blue. In the distance, it was almost too difficult to detect where the sea ended and the sky began. If it weren't for the slightly lighter shade the sky wore, the scene would have presented a nearly pure blue canvas framed by the plane's window. Out the window behind her, a few islands lay strewn about the water amidst besprinkled whitecaps; otherwise the sea was an unsullied baby blue. She gazed without purpose. Her eyes captured the scenery below and somehow enhanced it. Divine.

She stared out the window, saying her own private goodbyes to her vacation. She felt so relaxed and open. Her vacation had needed her, but she was also ready to return home. She hadn't had a real conversation with anyone for weeks. She hoped the seat beside her didn't remain empty on the flight.

As the seatbelt light turned off, she hummed the Patti Cline song that flowed through her headphones and pressed the button on her armrest to lean her chair back. A number of years ago she'd promised herself she would take a trip like this. She was so proud that she finally had the courage to do so. Life seemed to be closing in around her during the last few years. Her career had turned into a job, but she felt she had to keep pressing forward. It was the career at which she had been aiming for quite a while, so she couldn't just up and leave it. She drove the car she wanted and ate the foods she desired. She loved the home they had built together. Every day was, in fact, satisfying. Yet the totality of it all was suffocating. Maybe it was the fact that her life was now on a path that had been decided for her, and there was nothing more she could do. Almost like a deterministic deist would think about a higher power, she was coming to view her life with a similar sense of futility. It simply felt like there was nowhere for her to go. Even though the path she was currently on was the path that she had chosen and was most likely the path on which she hoped to follow in the future, she still felt trapped. So she hit the pause button and decided to fulfill the dream vacation she had always wanted, all by herself.

In her younger days she would have likely been too afraid to take this trip alone. In her years to come, as a middle-aged woman, she would probably recall with an aporetic smirk that she had once thought there were younger days before this flight. At this point in time, however, it was perfect. She felt a wisdom and a peace well beyond her years. Yet, she also felt a youthful exuberance that life had seemed to be slowly squeezing out of her. Her fingers laced together behind her head as she stared upward. The world seemed like such a simple place in this moment. *Worry is overrated*, she thought smiling. *Death is always approaching. Disappointment circles only when expectations guide the daily existence.* She was experiencing a calm that flowed through unstrained breath. When life was filled with mere substance, she now understood, only angst could follow. Yet when aspirations and restraint were ignored, aimlessness escorted her every step. At this point, she didn't care about any of it.

The stewardess smiled across the row to her and asked if she would like a beverage. "A water would be nice." She glowed. "And a chardonnay."

It was still vacation in her mind; why not continue to enjoy her newfound peace? The stewardess nodded and continued to smile. It was hard for the stewardess not to smile at her. She held a presence within in her that emanated accord. Finally the flight attendant continued moving through the rows, but the pleasant visage remained. The gentleman next to her rocked back and forth, not nervously, but in a honest manner, like a metronome. It was distracting to her because of the simplicity of its exactness. She was not disturbed or annoyed, but merely entranced. The gentleman's beard was a peppered gray and the hair on his head whiter than that. He was likely in his 60's. As she continued to glance at him, he finally looked over with a gentle smile. His rocking stopped, but the precise manner of his movements did not.

She removed her headphones to introduce herself, and the gentleman returned the nicety. Neither spoke for a moment until the man, accepting the opportunity, said, "You look well."

"Thanks," she replied. "I feel great. I have had the most wonderful time." She felt a silent invitation from the man to continue, and she obliged.

"I just took some time to get away. My life, my job, everything seemed to be closing in around me. This trip allowed me to find myself. I feel like a young girl again—full of wonder about what lies ahead and full of hope for what I can add to those around me. I feel excited to return again to what I left behind. You know, when I left I knew I had some great things, but I also knew I needed time to get away from all of them. I needed time to breathe easy. I remember when I was a child. Every day I was excited to wake up, so much so that I would roam through my house waking up my brothers and sisters. The sun each day seemed so inviting. Each night I hated going to bed. There was too much to do and so much to say. How could I go to sleep?

"I forgot what it felt like," she pressed. "I really do love my life, but I wasn't enjoying it anymore. Each morning I began to hate waking up. Each evening I couldn't wait to fall asleep. I once again feel like that little girl I was so long ago, bright-eyed and excited."

"What changed?" the gentleman patiently inquired.

"Me, I think. Time away. I changed by not changing anything about my life or even about myself. The only thing that really changed is probably my attitude toward it all. And the only thing that I needed was time. Life was swirling around, and I had become a spectator. The odd thing is that it required taking a vacation away from it all, a vacation where I was merely a spectator toward everything and everyone around me, for me to realize I wanted to be a participant again. I want to participate in life, not just watch it go by. But this time I want to be affected by, as much as I want to affect, the world around me. I don't know how to put it other than to say that I feel like a kid again. I want people to listen to me, but I want to listen to them just as much. I want the stars to remain a wonder, and the sea to remain powerful. I want a soufflé and a glass of Cabernet to make my taste buds jump. Most of all, I want my love to effervesce into an outpouring of new life. I want my new sense of self to bring happiness and peace to my love."

She hesitated a moment and shook her head. "I probably sound stupid," she said with a smile.

"No, not at all. You sound wonderful. So you have someone back home? You have a love?"

"I do," she glowed. "He has been the man that I have always dreamed of and wanted. He is strong and serious. Don't get me wrong, he knows how to have fun and really enjoys life. He is a staunch individual, though, that always does right by those around him. He has always loved me from the very first day we met. I still remember one of our very first dates. I had pushed away his advances for months before I finally gave in. He took me to a dingy bar. He felt comfortable in that type of setting. I listened to him share stories for what must have been hours. I didn't care that we were in a dive bar. It was wonderful. It was the dead of winter and freezing outside that night. We sat in that bustling bar, and my usually quiet-mannered husband shared story after story. He was clearly trying to impress me. We left the bar venturing into the cold hand-in-hand that night. That's when I knew I loved him, and I wanted to marry him."

"On one of your first dates?"

"Oh yes. There was no doubt in my mind as we left the bar that night. There are things I would like to change about him and our relationship, sure, but I wouldn't give him up for anything. I love him dearly." She paused for a moment to stare out the window. Their plane now soared above the clouds. "But enough about me. What about you? Why are you traveling?"

"I always travel," he said matter-of-factly, "but not by choice. Or at least not by a self-determined choice. I'm a traveler. A wanderer." His voice trailed off as he finished the sentence, but he never lost his measured tone. He let the words hang in the air.

She smiled at him, waiting for more of his untold story. He continued, "When I was a young man I didn't travel that much. I lived with my wife and son. We had a wonderful life."

"What happened?"

"Life happened," he paused as a sadness overtook him. "Our son passed in a hiking accident in Thailand. We were devastated. Our son was amazing. My wife and I just drifted apart after that. Our marriage wasn't strong enough to survive the death of our son."

"I'm so sorry," she said as she grabbed his hand. She squeezed it tightly as her eyes pierced his with concern. It was clear he did not want to discuss it anymore, and he moved on.

"We lived in a beautiful home. It was a turn-of-the-century Victorian with a magnificent wrap-around front porch." He paused, admiring the image in his mind. "God, I enjoyed sitting on that front porch. I would watch each passerby and smile at the sun. More than anything else, I would admire the oak tree in my front yard.

"That oak was a glorious work of nature. The house was nearly a hundred years old, and the tree must have been there twice as long. It towered above all the others on my tree-lined street. It was majestic in its presence. I admired everything about it. Its branches alone were the size of tree trunks. The neighborhood grew around it over the years, but the oak continued to stand tall and strong. I marveled at the patience it took that tree to become a beacon on the street—years upon years. The storms this tree must have weathered. The changes it witnessed. It was as if it took all the faults and the guilt of the neighborhood upon itself. The world evolved around it. All the while, the oak never wavered. It continued to grow and tower above everything.

"After years of admiring this oak, something slowly changed. I noticed a few minor changes at first. A few branches looked weaker than before. Each spring the leaves appeared less green than I remembered them being in previous years. But I convinced myself I was imagining things. To the unsuspecting eye, the oak looked as strong and glorious as ever. So I convinced myself I was merely misremembering the oak's magnificence out of a misguided nostalgia.

"One night during a storm, the oak began to shake. It wasn't a strong storm, just a light thunderstorm common in those parts throughout the summer months. Then, without warning, the majestic tree began to topple. The weight of the oak caused it to slowly tip. Loud muffled noises awoke me from my sleep, and I rushed out of my home. I scurried to my driveway to watch. Everything moved in slow motion, not because my mind slowed the moment down like a horrible car accident, but because the oak was actually tipping ever so slowly. The noises grew louder. Then I realized there was sound coming from beneath my feet. The roots had spread all the way to the driveway.

"I rushed across the street in time to watch the roots of this massive oak tree slowly rise from the ground. The sound was like a horrible discord, and it grew louder as the tree leaned closer to the earth. The light rain mixed with the oak's sap and dripped to the ground through the cracked limbs, as if sweat were pouring from the tree under the strain of trying to maintain its place on the street. It amazed me watching a tree that had been so strong over the years collapse to the earth. Ever so slowly the tree inched closer and closer to its death while the noises beneath it grew louder.

"As I stood across the street, the rain drizzled across my face; it was at that moment the groans from underneath the ground reached the surface. The cracking, gnashing, snapping...those roots tore from the earth with such force. So much destruction lay beneath the surface. These massive roots—roots I had never seen before in my life, never even contemplated their existence—destroyed everything in their vicinity. The lawn around the tree was destroyed. The beautiful flower garden I had spent time on was ripped apart. Parts of the street and the neighbors' lawns were torn asunder. The saddest, though, was that front porch. When I watched those massive roots tear apart that porch, my heart sank. I sat down on the curb across from my home and stared in disbelief. I was devastated, watching the home I had worked on for so long being torn apart.

"I remember the police and fire trucks arriving sometime after. They talked to me for a bit, but I couldn't believe the front of my home had been destroyed. After a while, I stared in a trance and asked one of the officers how this could have happened. You know what he said to me?" The man tried to smile, but all he could muster was a doleful smirk.

"No," she replied. "What caused the oak to fall?"

The man's measured intonation finally broke as he shrugged his shoulders. "Neglect. Not neglect on my part nor neglect by previous owners of the land, but neglect by the oak itself. My precious oak had no longer been diligent about where it laid down its roots. The officer told me that the tree had been wrapping its roots around rotten ground for years. The entire time this massive front-yard pillar towered over the neighborhood, it had been driving is roots into rotten dirt. It was only a matter of time before it tumbled. The tree itself was as strong as ever, but the very soil it continued to drive its roots into was rotten. It's amazing it stood so tall and strong as long as it actually did. While towering high above the ground, below the surface the oak was as weak as a poisoned, dying tree."

The man stroked his white and black beard as he stared at the back of the seat. His eyes glazed over for a long while as he remained lost in a memory. Then he continued abruptly.

"Insurance covered some of the destruction to my house and yard, but it was never the same for me. It never could be. I made plans to rebuild that beautiful porch, but by that point, it had lost its wonder. Like that poor oak, the porch would never be the same. So I sold the place and left. Been traveling ever since..." He again trailed off.

She tried to imagine that beautiful porch that the man had loved so dearly. She thought about their front porch back home that she and her husband both loved so dearly. They had restored it to pristine condition. Everyone in the neighborhood loved their porch in all its perfection.

"Have you ever been back?" she whispered. "You know, to see if the porch was ever rebuilt?"

"No," he replied faintly. "It can never be rebuilt."

Then he leaned his chair back. "It's time for me to sleep," he said without expression. With that, he closed his eyes.

She finished her last drink of Chardonnay and decided to sleep herself. She took the sleeping pill in her pocket and drank it down with her last gulp of water. The story resonated in her thoughts for a while as she tried to picture the scene the man had described. Soon, however, she was dreaming that she sat high above the ground in a tree house. She was bird watching. Beautiful long-winged creatures soared about her, arrogantly strutting their majestic colors. Her plane soared onward home.

FOUR

The sun shone brightly again today. Instead of going directly home after work, he decided to wander through town for a bit. He was so hot he wanted to remove his shirt, but he thought it would be indecent to walk through the populated area without it. So he continued to sweat in the heat. He almost felt suffocated. As he walked through town, he held his head high. He always did. Never stare at the ground below you, he was taught. Always look straight ahead. A few passersby nodded, and he returned the gesture. A little girl bumped into him. She couldn't have been higher than his thigh. She looked up at him and then immediately scurried behind her father. He smiled kindly at her father. Not a word was exchanged as the father picked his daughter up, and she buried her face into his chest. He smiled again, this time at the paternal exchange. Someday maybe.

He paused for a moment in the shade of a store awning. He saw a necklace in the window that he thought was beautiful. *She wouldn't like it though*, he thought. It was too gaudy, and the jade stones looked cheap. But the color sparkled in the store window. He couldn't pull himself away for a moment. The deep teal reminded him of days on the ocean shore. He loved the ocean—the salt air brushing against his face, the sand in his toes, and the rolling waves flowing onto the shore, never ending. He couldn't help but to sit and think deeply when he sat on the ocean shore. His thoughts drifted to anything and everything as he stared off into the horizon. He had been longing for a trip to the ocean for a while. They had actually planned a trip together a year ago or so, but they kept pushing it back. Things were always too busy. There were always bills to pay. Life kept getting in the way of living.

One day she approached him and said she needed to get away. She needed some time to recollect herself and focus her life. "Not long," she said. But time is relative, and distance can either drive a wedge or draw together. He smiled at her, and he knew she was right. She needed to refocus her life on what mattered most to her. He didn't withhold his agreement to her idea for even a second. "Take some time to yourself," he remembered saying. "You deserve every bit of it. Everyone needs a retreat every once in a while."

He could tell how appreciative she was. She had thought this might be a battle, or even worse, that he might be deeply hurt by her taking some time away for herself. She was ecstatic to see his immediate approval. She hugged him as he held her close. He remembered now how they had talked for hours about where might be the best place for her to get away. They both seemed to agree that it should be somewhere warm and tropical. Eventually, she fell asleep on the couch with her head in his lap. He ran his fingers through her golden hair as he sipped the end of his can of beer. He feared the day he would be left alone on that couch.

As he continued to stare into the necklace, he lingered, thinking about the ocean. Oh, how he missed it. "I hope she's happy," he mumbled. And while anyone passing by may have doubted the sincerity of his remark, the sentiment was heartfelt and true. He pictured her on the beach with the waves rolling into the shore. He'd always marveled at the ocean waves. They reminded him of his life. The waves of life never ceased rolling onto the shore. Sometimes they were so big that they would knock him off his feet. Other times they were hardly noticeable. If he didn't move from one spot for a while, the waves would slowly erode the sand underneath his feet, and he would be six inches deep. But the waves never stopped coming. Always rolling in. Sometimes crashing, sometimes not, but never ceasing. He had learned at a young age that he couldn't wait for those waves to stop. If he did, he would always be waiting. He had to perdure. If a wave knocked him over, he got back up. If his legs grew tired from the constant blow of the water, he changed his angle or slowed his pace, but he never stopped. He learned early that those who stopped sank; those who rested drowned.

Finally he stepped away from the window and back into the beating sunlight. He wiped the sweat from his brow and rolled his shoulders to relax his back as he stared up at the sky. When he began walking again, he threw a polite gaze toward an elderly woman walking past. Despite the heat, she had on a long dress and a light gray sweater covering her arms. *She must be warm,* he thought. He couldn't tell if she noticed his greeting, but that was fine.

In the distance he saw a young boy sprinting after a collie that was rapidly approaching with its leash flailing about behind it. He placed himself in front of the fleeing dog and grabbed her before she could run off. The dog readily accepted his greeting and jumped onto its hind legs into his arms. She licked his face a few times before he settled her down and grabbed the leash. He offered a neighborly grin and handed the boy the leash. The boy grabbed the leash and went on his way running down the street relieved, without a word of thanks.

He spat on the ground and grumbled something about youth these days, only because he thought the words to be fitting, not because he actually believed them. He frowned automatically as he continued to nod at those he passed. The heat was unceasing. His shirt was soaked through from another long day's work. He looked at the sidewalk below and noticed how nicely it had been paved. Just a year ago, nearly every slab was cracked and uneven. Now, each storefront looked pristine. The young trees that lined the main street remained intact with the sidewalk improvements. A few new trees had been planted as well. The town was picturesque and wistful for some, small and suffocating for others. It was all a matter of the beholder's gaze. Signs for antique shops, diners, and craft stores made up most of the storefronts. A strong old man swept a store's entrance. He nodded approvingly to the old man as he passed.

He glanced at his watch blankly and thought he should drive home. Crossing the street, he saw a young man hopelessly ignoring the world around him as he sat on a stoop in front of the local barber's shop. In the man's eyes seemed to rest the acrimony of the world. A small styrofoam cup sat beside him. Most people passing by might mistake the nearly empty cup for a cup of coffee, if it weren't so hot and the young man didn't look so pathetically alone. He felt drawn to the young man sitting there alone on the street as if pulled by an unseen force to appease his suffering.

He walked directly toward the barbershop and pulled out a five-dollar bill. He waited patiently for the young man to look up at him. When their eyes met, he crouched down and stuck his hand out. The young man took the money. He shook the young man's hand as the vagrant placed the five dollars into the cup. The two gazed at each other for another brief moment. He noticed the young man's eyes come to life ever so slightly, and he smiled kindly in return. Neither said a word. He rose to his feet and continued his walk back to his truck.

....

FIVE

The baggage claim area buzzed with excited travelers returning home and disgruntled airline patrons hopelessly waiting for their bags. As each new piece of luggage peaked over the conveyer belt before it descended downward to the carousel, every waiting person examined it in careful anticipation, only to be left with further dissatisfaction when they realized it wasn't their bag. To her delight, however, her bag bounded down the belt and slid gracefully onto the carousel. She grabbed her suitcase and rolled it behind her. She hadn't even waited at the baggage claim for two minutes before it had arrived.

She smiled peacefully. The conversation from the flight stuck in the back of her mind. Why couldn't the man rebuild the porch? Why couldn't he have started over again? She couldn't shake the thought that he said he's a traveler, but not by choice. What did he mean by that? He chose to be a traveler.

The thoughts continued to race as she remembered the beautiful oak and how it tumbled. She thought about how her friend on the plane, recalling the rain and sap dripping from the tree as if the tree were sweating from the strain. She couldn't help but consider, now knowing the tree's fate, that it wasn't as if the oak were sweating, but bleeding as it fell to its demise, or maybe even crying. She pondered the man's anthropomorphic analogy while she dragged her luggage behind her. A woman leaving the bathroom nearly bumped into her. The woman immediately apologized and stepped to the side. She smiled at the woman politely as she passed.

She stopped off at the restroom, her thoughts hopeful for the weeks and months to come. She felt excited about her newfound appreciation toward even the ordinary. Good things were around the next corner. It wasn't as if things beforehand had not been good, but instead, that she had most likely not understood that they had been good. This made all the difference. Her cognizance of the beauty and joy around her enhanced even the simplest things. As she washed her hands, she stared glowingly in the mirror. The anticipation of her everyday duties, impelling exploits to be experienced, now enthralled her. She felt like she had been roaming blindly for the last few years, and now the scales had been removed from her eyes. This was a youthful exuberance she hadn't felt since her days back in school.

As she exited the restroom, she slowly surveyed the area, looking for the nearest taxi stand. When she found it, there was almost a skip in her first step towards the door. A middle-aged lady stumbled and then paused directly in front of her as she regained her balance. She waited patiently for the woman to proceed on her way, which she did after a few moments, but not before the maladroit woman looked up at her with a long glower of irritation. She wasn't sure if the woman somehow thought that she had tripped her, but she didn't worry about it too long. The woman glared for another beat and then went on her way. She smiled again pleasantly in the woman's direction without the slightest recognition in return.

Her bag in tow behind her, the doors to the outside parted automatically, and she marched through with purpose. The force of the heat hit her immediately, and she paused a moment. Then she strolled to the taxi stand to catch a ride home.

....

SIX

Another long day had engulfed him. He laboriously paced through the hours at work. The heat was as unyielding as the days before. It never seemed to bother him, though—at least not more than any other thing that may be bothersome. He trudged through the day as dutifully as on any other day. There certainly wasn't an overabundant sense of joy for the long days he spent at work, but who has such affection for manual labor? He wouldn't find a love for his work until he became a high school teacher years later. For now, he simply worked construction. "It's a living," he would say.

After this particularly long day of work, he drove out to his favorite spot on the countryside. After following the winding highway, he turned down the dirt road as dust kicked up around him. It was too hot to roll up the windows, and the dust began to get in his eyes, so he slowed down. Oak trees flanked the road with a few birch thrown in for good measure. He always felt at ease when he hit the country roads. He looked content as he took a long drink of an unlabeled dark jar of liquid.

He parked the car at the end of a long grove of trees. Before him lay an expansive field. While the dusk sky faded to black, he stared ahead with a clear mind. He turned off his phone, escaping from the harsh world around him. He rested in the front seat for a while before climbing out of the car. His lungs breathed in the air with a deep heave, despite the thick humidity that still permeated. A large red pebble, out of place on the dirt road, caught his eye. He picked it up. His gaze momentarily fixated on its smooth contours and the deep hue of red. He briefly smiled, recalling a memory from another time. Then he tossed the stone into the field and walked to the front of the truck.

He lay on the hood, paint chipping on all corners of the truck. His head rested on the windshield. The night sky above was radiant, as if angels were gathering the stars just for him. He had driven an hour into the country for no particular reason at all. There was not a city light to be seen. The stars glowed across the expansive dark canvas that acted as their backdrop. Ursa Major welcomed the hundreds of additional, resplendent bursts of light into its constellation. These stars, some dim and some robust, accentuated the certainty of the Big Dipper. They were simply guests at the soiree that the constellation hosted across the night sky. Orion, on the other hand, appeared less welcoming. Every star that customarily remained clandestine to the city stargazer currently pronounced its existence. The bold and breathtaking multitude simply overwhelmed Orion. It was nearly impossible to spot even the three ever-present stars that made up the warrior's belt. After peering upwards for a while, though, he spotted the belt. It just refused to be as conspicuous as one might suspect. The sheer plenitude of stars was heart stirring.

Amidst all the splendor, the moon hung regally, not high in the sky nor low on the horizon either. It was not full and demanding attention in its brightness, and it was not waning to the point of only appearing as God's fingernail. It just hung, another member of the party. The sky knew of its existence, though; that was for certain. The canvas above adhered to the moon's presence as much as the moon affixed itself to the stars around it. The night sun never overpowered the rest of the composition, but it left a noble ring in its immediate vicinity that no stars dared to encroach. The moon unknowingly demanded the attention of everything in its presence.

And yet, he didn't seem to notice. His gaze was transfixed upwards, but his attention to it seemed fleeting. His mind was far from the commanding presence that the sky held.

His stare was blank and painstakingly empty. His bold eyes welled for just an instant. Once again, his brow furrowed. The moment hung in the air. There was a deep longing within him that wanted to escape. A constant yearning to know that what he was doing, that what he did, was valuable. He could blithely carry every burden that presented itself if he only knew that there was meaning in his tribulation. He didn't care about acceptance. That's not what he wanted at all. He wanted appreciation. He wanted to know that his daily struggles were not in vain. He needed to know that his continuous strife was more than that. He needed to know that she was better because of it. He longed to understand that his sacrifice made her more complete. If he had that, he would be content. The moon hung in the air with the moment.

He lifted the drink in his hand to his lips. A long, forced drink flowed. He lay across the front of his old truck, which had long been discontinued by the manufacturer. It was wide and drove low to the ground like a boat. He loved that old truck. The jar in his hand once again casually touched his dry lips, and he took a swig. He always saved the mason jars that had originally contained pasta sauce or pickles. He would clean them thoroughly more than once, and then he would store them on a shelf in the kitchen for re-use. She had always asked him why he would meticulously clean and save every single jar when there were clearly more than enough jars on the shelf already. "I just want to, I suppose," he would retort. It was something he enjoyed doing. He couldn't remember the specifics of what now filled the jar he was currently holding, but it was dark—a whiskey or a bourbon—and it was strong. Really strong. He took another drink. The moon hung, but the moment passed.

....

SEVEN

The heat was oppressive. It wasn't merely the ever-increasing temperature, but the humidity. It hung on her like a wet blanket as she approached the taxi stand. After a pleasant, warm heat for weeks, and the ability to slide into the ocean water to cool off whenever the slightest discomfort would arise, this summer heat was sweltering. Each breath took a little more effort and required her to breathe in a little deeper. The temperature, in fact, had dropped from earlier in the week, and the humidity had eased its grip. If there ever were dog days, they were the couple of days prior. Nonetheless, she was not prepared for this onslaught.

The attendant at the taxi stand said nothing, mostly due to the fact that the attendant had been replaced by an electronic pay-stand a few months ago. No longer was there a polite gentleman greeting her as she approached, inquiring about her long journey. The days of those niceties and a cordial opening of the taxi door were gone. Instead, she inserted her credit card into the machine and waited for a receipt to print. *What's temporally efficient is not always efficient for the soul*, she thought.

She grabbed her receipt from the machine and spun around to find a middle-aged man beaming at her. The excitement he had as he reached for her luggage was palpable. She couldn't help but smile back at her driver, although it wasn't as if her smile had really faded at all since she had landed. He placed her bags in the trunk and quickly raced around to the side of the cab just in time to open the rear driver's door for her. She was amused by this unexpected chivalry and acquiesced to the gesture, gently sliding into the back seat. He quickly assumed his position in control of the vehicle and directed the cab out of the airport.

He smiled into the rearview mirror. His gaze held a little too long before he blurted, "Coming home?"

"Yes," she responded politely.

Her weeks away reminded her how much she enjoyed people. She used to always welcome conversations with strangers. In fact, when she had been younger, she would always recall how Mother Teresa once said that she'd never left a conversation without learning at least one thing about the world. She used to love this sentiment and strove to put it into practice. Over the years, though, it had become a bear. Time was too short, and people were not interesting enough, at least that's what she had come to believe. After her trip, she had a renewed vigor for people and what they had to say. Her taxi driver's interest in her travels was welcome.

"Where from?"

"Oh...away," she smiled. "Beach, sleep, mimosas and me. It was wonderful."

"Good for you, Miss. Good for you. Everyone should take time for themselves."

"Mmmhmm. I needed it too. My life had taken on its own existence. I needed to regain control."

He merged onto the freeway and nodded approvingly. She reached into her bag and grabbed her cell phone. She hadn't touched the thing for weeks. Not more than a month ago, she would have felt naked had she left the house without it. It caused her anxiety to shut it off when she first left on her vacation. She would walk the beach and instinctively check her bag for her phone. If a moment slowed, as when she waited in line for a gyro, she would reach for her phone without thinking. After a few days, however, she had walked the streets freely without it. She laughed at the thought of feeling naked without her phone, as if she were walking around topless, embarrassed with shame. It was the Emperor's New Clothes for a new generation. With her phone at her fingertips, she had felt protected and clothed, even though the clothing was a mirage. Pure folly. Now the thing felt foreign in her hands. Cold. Awkward. She zipped her bag closed, putting the phone into her purse without turning it on. Just a little longer, she beamed.

"Excuse me, Miss. Forgive me, but I must say, you look strikingly like my sister."

"Oh?"

"Yes. She was beautiful like you. Long blonde hair, deep blue eyes, and could stop a room with her smile."

"Well, thank you."

"No, thank you, Miss. I'm filled with emotion just looking at you," he said as he eased the cab out of traffic and toward the off-ramp. "When we were younger, I was shy. I couldn't enter a room without immediately looking for the nearest corner to hide in. My sister used to put her arm around me and march us right into the room. The mood in the room would immediately change when she entered it. People would beam with excitement when they saw her. They would jump up to say hello and give her a hug. And there I was under my sister's arm. She introduced me to a world I would have never known. She was my everything."

The past tense of his words hung in the air. "My sister died almost five years ago," he continued solemnly. "Cancer. It took her looks first. The blue in her eyes faded quickly after that. It was heart wrenching for me. I begged God to let the cancer pass and to leave her be. She always consoled me that it was going to be okay, that this was her fate and she accepted it. I felt incredibly feeble that my sister needed to be the one consoling me. It wouldn't have been my will, for the cancer to deteriorate her body like that, but she never seemed to question it. It was as if she knew there wasn't any other way her life could be coming to an end. Somehow, through it all, the cancer couldn't touch her smile. Her smile never left, no matter how painful that cancer was. Hope, ya know?" He paused momentarily, not particularly waiting for an answer.

"For a while after she passed, I struggled to move on. I went back to being a loner. I lost hope in everything. Somewhere along the way, though, her smile came back to me. The hope that had eluded me after she died slowly came back. It came back every time I thought of that smile of hers. It was such a beautiful smile. I try to always take it with me now."

The taxi turned down her street and slowed to a halt. The young man slowed the car to a stop and turned around. "I'm sorry. It was just a pleasure to drive you. Sometimes, life offers unexpected gifts, don't it? I'm sorry to burden you, though."

"Nonsense," she calmly responded. "I'm sure I'm nowhere near as wonderful as your sister was. She sounds like she was an impressive individual. I wish I could have had the chance to meet her. But I had the chance to meet you, and you're extraordinary."

She paid the driver, and the man smiled kindly to her. She reached out her hand and placed it on his shoulder.

"Thank you for sharing your sister with me. Hold her smile in your heart every day. Let it fill your heart until you can't contain it any longer. Then, when there's no room left in your heart for her smile, let it burst out of you, and share her smile with the world."

She smiled, rubbed his shoulder, and exited the cab with her bags.

As she strode up the front walk, the driver slowly inched away. He turned down the next street, parked his car, and wept.

....

EIGHT

His final drink from the mason jar was a long one. The alcohol was strong, but his face remained expressionless. The moon had pushed its way across the night sky. The stars obliged and moved with it, a glorious dance across the sky. The moon now hung high in the sky with the all the stars gathered around it. The understated moon had become the center of attention, and it had done so swiftly.

He thought about the times he stared at the night sky with her. He longed to watch the stars again with her, wishing she was by his side right now, wishing she had an hour to watch the night sky with him.

He had turned his phone off hours ago. He slid down the front of his truck fumbling the mason jar. It bounced off the bumper and shattered, not into countless pieces, but into four jagged pieces. The largest piece, still maintaining most of the shape and the body of the jar, fell to the ground with two other pieces of glass. The fourth piece lay wedged between the bumper and the grill. "Damn it," he muttered. He bent over, placing the two broken pieces on the ground into what remained of the jar. Reaching for the sharp piece of glass wedged in the bumper, he jerked unexpectedly. His hand lunged a little too far, cutting his middle finger.

"Shhhhii—," he trailed off. He put his now bloody finger into his mouth. He scowled at the piece of glass when he picked it up with his other hand and forced it into the jar with the others.

As he climbed back into the truck, the blood slowly seeped from his middle finger into his mouth. He couldn't remember the last time he tasted blood. What did it taste like? He slowly swallowed the traces of blood that oozed from his finger. It tasted like...blood. He set the broken jar on the floor of the passenger seat and angrily started the car.

"Damn it," he mumbled again.

He thought about the last time he could remember tasting blood. It shouldn't be rare for someone in construction like himself to experience small cuts, but the last time he could remember was when he was a child. He was in grade school on the playground. A friend had brought a pocketknife to school to show off to his friends. He could still remember the knife—bright red and shiny as a fire truck. It had two or three gadgets, but the knife was the centerpiece. It was dazzling contraband for a little kid on the playground.

The next day a schoolyard skirmish broke out. Name calling escalated to minor shoving, at which point his friend pulled out the pocketknife as a joke, trying to ease the tension. He called his friend an idiot and went to push his arm aside, but his friend motioned with the knife at the same time. The blade sliced across his knuckle, and blood immediately poured out. His friend started crying. He simply stared blankly, slightly stunned, while he placed the new bleeding cut into his mouth. Soon the nuns that monitored the schoolyard descended upon them. Detentions were given out in the aftermath. No recess for him, his friend, and the others for two weeks. That was the last time he could remember tasting blood.

He eased the truck off the dirt road and back onto the two-lane highway. It was dark on the road. Nearly pitch black. His middle finger had decided to subside its bleeding, and he placed both hands on the wheel. The bright lights of an oncoming car caused him to squint for a moment in an effort to make out the road ahead. As the car passed, he glanced to the floor next to him and shook his head at the jar.

"Stupid," he mumbled, looking back at his finger.

When his eyes returned to the road, he realized he was riding the centerline. He quickly jerked the car to the right, overcompensating and gliding into the gravel on the shoulder. Eventually the car righted back to the road. He rubbed his liquored eyes, narrowing his vision to focus on the road.

The truck turned the corner to his street a little too fast. He slowed the vehicle to nearly a crawl before realizing how slowly he was moving. In a confused attempt to approach his driveway in a normal manner, he sped up and cut the turn too sharply. The wheels screeched on the front walk and clipped a rose in the front bed. He screeched to a halt and shut off the engine abruptly. The silence jolted him. He stared at his house. *She should be home soon*, he thought. His heart raced with excitement for an instant. Things seemed right when she was around. He needed her around.

The instant followed with a pang. The sadness of recent weeks washed over him. The bitterness of recent years engulfed him. He sighed deeply, and then noticing his finger, he once again mumbled to himself. He reached for the broken jar and exited the motionless vehicle.

As he stumbled up the front stairs, his shoe slipped, and he caught himself with his free hand. Fumbling the keys into the door, he opened the locked house. The place was dark, except for the kitchen light, which he had left on in the morning. He walked down the hall to the kitchen trash. He glanced at the clock, which glowered 2:55—a time that he knew was not only late, but also incorrect. It was just about seven minutes later than the clock reported. He reached below the kitchen sink to pull the cupboard door open. When he reached in to toss his broken jar, he once again saw the letter. He gently laid the broken pieces on the letter. His eyes welled up. His head hung.

....

NINE

Hours earlier she had exited her cab driver's taxi and watched him slowly pull away. She smiled gracefully as he eased down the street, and then she turned into her home. Bound-

ing up the stairs, she left her bags on the front
walk. Disappointed to find the home locked, she
searched her purse for her keys. As the door swung
open, she timidly said hello with excitement. She
knew full well that he was likely not home from
work yet. Still, she was disappointed he wasn't
there. After delaying her return twice because she
was enjoying herself so much, she told him she had
finally decided to return to him, refreshed and relaxed. Her last letter said she would be back tomorrow morning, but she had changed her flight to
avoid a red-eye.

She softly called out to him again and searched
the front room. Nothing.

"No problem," she exhaled. Still beaming, she
bounded back down the front steps to grab her
luggage. This time she noticed the empty driveway
and shook her head at her own absent-mindedness.
"Of course he's not here," she moaned.

Returning up the steps, she paused on the front
porch. A big smile crept across her face as she
gazed at the columns—undeniably perfect, certainly the pride of the block, she thought. Neighbors
had expressed their appreciation of the restored
beauty of the porch multiple times. Every time it
happened, she glowed. She was humble in her response—"It's getting there,"—but inside she radiat-

ed a fulfilling pride. She loved those columns. They were perfect.

After showering and getting dressed, he had still not arrived. She excitedly sent a text, spilling the beans on her surprise: "Home early. Excited!"

She placed her phone back on the counter and decided to do her hair and makeup. She was filled with anticipation. So much had happened. There were no stories, but she had gone on a journey. In the commotion of the world, she had found peace. She wouldn't call it enlightenment, especially because she knew the transition would be difficult now that she was back home. But she knew she had changed. Her heart was filled with renewed strength. Beating with a new sense of love, she felt like a young teenager again. One individual can't change the world, but one individual can change another individual's world. She looked forward to sharing her newfound love with those around her. She smiled with excitement. She couldn't wait to tell him. He would be so happy for her.

She grabbed an apple from the fridge and took a bite. Over an hour had passed since she had climbed out of the shower. She was worried he might have headed to a bar after a long hot day, so she gave him a call. The text and the call ruined the surprise, but her excitement couldn't be contained.

Voicemail. She effusively broke the news again and told him to hurry home.

As the hours continued to pass, her excitement faded to disappointment. She continually checked her phone for a message or a missed call. She couldn't wait to tell him how she felt. He had always been kind to each person he met. "There is good in every man," he would often say. "Everyone has a story and a pain they fight. Don't judge them because you saw a moment when the pain overcame them and you saw a bad side of them. There's good in there."

She knew he would appreciate her experience while she was away. The renewed life in her bubbled up. He would nod, quietly approving. She didn't even know if she could express what she felt. This wasn't uncommon, though. She often struggled to find the words that would succinctly articulate her thoughts and emotions. Instead, she would shed words rapidly in hopes that one would hit the mark. As always, he would listen, nodding approvingly.

"I'm out of my mind," she would usually giggle after she would finish her most fervent speeches.

"No, I am," he would respond, leaning in to kiss her.

Her disappointment grew as the night waned. She looked around the house multiple times to see if there was a note or some kind of indication of where he might be. She over-analyzed the placement of a shoe. A bar of soap placed on the bathroom sink instead of the shower caused her to ponder its meaning. She, of course, knew they meant nothing, but she needed to pass the time. She fought feelings of betrayal by him, but the fleeting thoughts came, despite knowing she was merely trying to cover her own disappointment.

Finally, around midnight she sat down on the couch in the front room. She was worried something might have happened. Although her better senses told her he was fine, she was still worried.

He must have gotten my message. Why hasn't he come home? Despite her disappointment, she patiently waited. *I knew surprising him was a bad idea,* she thought.

After dozing in and out of sleep on the couch, she heard a tire screech outside. She sat up straight, jolted awake. There wasn't movement outside for what felt like minutes, until the truck door at long last slammed shut. She watched him stumble through the door and then down the hall past the entryway of the front room where she sat. She smiled as a tear rolled down her cheek. Her kindness remained despite overwhelming disappointment. Glass clinked in the kitchen, and a cupboard door shut. Then silence. She clicked on the light next to her.

....

TEN

The moment the light turned on, he froze. His thoughts raced as he tried to gather himself. He leaned on the counter in front of him to regain his balance. *Who was here?* he thought as his body stiffened with athletic rigidity. He was as ready to defend and protect his family and his home as he always was. Then his muscles relaxed. He knew. He didn't need to turn on his phone and check for the missed calls and texts. He knew. His face brightened ever so slightly. A smile crept across him, and his eyes moistened. He paused a moment, then he slowly walked back down the hall.

She continued to wait on the couch. She hadn't stirred, but had listened while he had stood motionless in the kitchen. Then she heard his footsteps down the hall. They were even and tempered. Each step followed the other in exact tempo, like a metronome. Her stomach immediately filled with simultaneous butterflies and anxiety. His steps continued in measured beat for so long that the hallway must have grown four sizes in length while she was away. After each soft thump on the floor, she anticipated his silhouette appearing in the threshold before her.

Finally, there he stood. His weary head hung like a child unable to support the weight. His eyes stared meekly at the floor.

He leaned against the door. The agony of the last few weeks flooded his thoughts. She frowned at him for a moment, but then her kind smile returned. It took a beat before he raised his gaze to her. In his eyes was a mix of yearning and sadness. He longed for her. He had longed for her every minute she had been away. He wanted to feel her gentleness, the mercy she brought upon him with her kind smile. She wanted the same.

She met his forlorn gaze. An immediate mixture of anguish and hope overcame her from deep within.

"I missed you, Al."

"I missed you too, Maria."

Their eyes locked upon each other. Neither one said anything for minute.

"Love, I'm sorry."

"What for? I'm yours, and that's it. Whatever."
"I should not have been gone for so long."
"I'm yours, and that's it. Forever."
"You're mine, and that's it. Forever."

ACKNOWLEDGEMENTS

I am deeply grateful for the love, support, and wisdom offered by countless people that have helped to make this book a reality. I have been blessed with wonderful teachers, mentors, and family in my life, all of whom have shaped pieces of me. To all of you, I am grateful. I would be remiss if I did not acknowledge a number of individuals specifically.

Jon Balsbaugh: Your "101 College Tips" inspired the concept used in Expect Dragons. Thank you for always inspiring our high school class years ago.

Victor Davis: Thank you for excellent edits and sharp feedback.

Laura Buri, Paul Lamers, and Matt Miller: Thank you for taking the time to read my stories and provide insightful feedback on ways to improve them.

David Mattox: Your photography is amazing. You have an eye for light and composition. Thank you for providing the brilliant cover photograph. Thank you also for your thoughtful and critical suggestions on how to improve these stories. I appreciate your support throughout this process.

John and Kathy: You are amazing parents. I am blessed beyond words to have been raised and taught by you both. Thank you for your countless hours of editing, reviewing, encouraging, and enjoying my stories. This book would not be a reality without you both. You have taught me how to take risks and follow my passions.

Isla: At only two years old, I am awestruck by how much you have already taught me. Thank you for reminding me to explore with tenacity, laugh with abandon, cry with passion, and hope with grace. Never lose your sense of wonder.

Sara: You have watched me explore a passion for story telling for over a decade now. I can only imagine the frustration a lesser woman would have with my countless hours of writing, revising, editing, and worrying; but you have been beacon of grace and encouragement. Thank you for your suggestions, they improved the stories greatly. Thank you for your endless love and support. But most of all, thank you for being my best friend and companion in this life.

ABOUT THE AUTHOR

Dan Buri's first collection of short fiction, *Pieces Like Pottery*, is an exploration of heartbreak and redemption that announces the arrival of a new American author. His writing is uniquely heartfelt and explores the depths of the human struggle and the human search for meaning in life.

Mr. Buri's non-fiction works have been distributed online and in print, including publications in Pundit Press, Tree, Summit Avenue Review, American Discovery, and TC Huddle. The defunct and very well regarded Buris On The Couch, was a He-

Says/She-Says blog musing on the ups and downs of marriage with his wife.

Mr. Buri is an active patent attorney in the Pacific Northwest and has been recognized by Intellectual Asset Magazine as one of the World's Top 300 Intellectual Property Strategists every year since 2010. He lives in Oregon with his wife and two-year-old daughter

CPSIA information can be obtained
at www.ICGtesting.com
Printed in the USA
FSOW01n0457151216
28592FS